PLAIN INFERNO

ALISON STONE

TREEHAVEN PRESS

PLAIN INFERNO
Treehaven Press

Rev.C

❀ Created with Vellum

CHAPTER 1

Jeb King's cell phone dinged on the bedside table. He glanced over at Tessa, his sleeping wife, while simultaneously palming the phone. Pushing up onto one elbow, he blinked at the screen to clear his blurry eyes. The text message made his heart jolt.

Go now! They're headed your way.

He bolted upright. The quilt fell from his bare chest, exposing him to the cold air in the drafty cabin. He didn't recognize the number but he suspected he knew who "they" were.

Who would warn him? Was it a trap?

Realizing time was a luxury he didn't have, he slipped out of bed. He held his breath, hoping he could get dressed and out of the house without waking his wife. He didn't want to risk another argument.

"What is it?" Tessa asked sleepily, and he hated that he had grown to resent her. She had no business questioning him. *He* was the man of the house. *He* knew what had to be done.

Sucking in a breath, he turned to face her and forced an insincere smile. The white moonlight cut across her porcelain skin; her eyes studied him warily. He remembered a time not that long ago when she gazed upon him with nothing but love and admiration. Now her pretty brown eyes narrowed with crushing disappointment.

Or maybe you're projecting.

How had he failed so miserably? At everything.

"What's going on?" she asked again when he didn't answer. She scooted up to a seated position and leaned against the headboard his father had handcrafted before alcohol became his favorite pastime. She shoved her long wavy brown hair from her face. "Are you okay?"

"I'm fine," he lied as a blanket of pinpricks raced across his flesh. "Eddie has another job for me."

"A job? Now? In the middle of the night?" Tessa pulled up her legs and hugged her knees to her chest under the quilt.

The urge to confess welled up inside him. He had messed up. Big time. But doing so would only put her in danger. "Yeah, yeah…don't worry." Jeb snagged his pants from the chair where he had discarded them last night.

"What time is it?" she asked, leaning over to snag her watch from the nightstand.

"Late. Go back to sleep." He turned and grabbed his shirt and pulled it over his head.

"Jeb, what is it?" Her question held more sympathy than he deserved.

"Nothing. Nothing." Jeb pressed a kiss to her forehead. He paused and found himself frozen, memorizing this moment. He loved her long brown hair flowing over her shoulders, wavy from the braids she always wore. The first time he had met Tessa, she had braids wrapped around her head, probably a habit from growing up Amish. Or maybe it was easier to keep her hair that way so she could slip back into her Amish home late at night without her parents knowing she was hanging out with *Englisch* boys.

Hanging out with him.

A lifetime ago.

"Everything's fine. Just want to make money so you can have nice things."

Tessa reached up and caught his hand. "I have everything I need." This had been their ongoing argument during their short marriage. Jeb wanted more than this cramped cabin, the same one where he had grown up. Tessa was content.

"I'll take the snowmobile over to the bridge where Eddie will pick me up." The road to their cabin needed a good plowing out before being accessible. His junky little car would never make it. "When I'm done, I'll bring back breakfast sandwiches from the diner, okay?" He hated deceiving her, but he had to protect her. The people he was running from didn't have a beef with her. If he left, they'd come looking for him. Not her. She was innocent in all this.

He had done it for her. For them.

For their future.

But he feared he had overplayed his hand.

"Okay, be careful," she said, then laid back down and pulled the blanket over her shoulder.

Jeb stared at her for a moment longer then finished dressing quickly, putting on warm socks and all his winter gear. He slipped his cell phone into his jacket pocket. If they came by the house, they'd see his tracks. He'd lead them away from Tessa. Then he'd toss the cell phone into the creek and make his getaway. No way to track him.

Then what? He couldn't think straight. *Then what?*

There would be no breakfast sandwiches this morning. He prayed he could come back for his wife. Eventually. There had to be a way, but he hadn't figured it out yet despite sleepless nights racking his brain.

A so-called brilliant idea to earn some cash had turned out to be the dumbest thing he had done in his life. And he had done a lot of dumb things during his formative years after his father bailed and his mother died. His older brother, Sawyer, tried to rein him in, but life was more fun without rules. And why bother toeing the line when he'd never had to suffer the consequences?

Until now.

Jeb lumbered across the yard, his boots punching holes in the deep snow. He snagged the go-bag he had hidden in the garage among the disintegrating cardboard boxes containing memories from his parents' lives. He wondered why he hadn't chucked them out years ago.

Jeb secured the bag to the back of his snowmobile. It wasn't much, but it would hold him over until he figured out how to come back for Tessa when it was safe. He straddled the sled and started it up. The engine echoed in the winter night, disturbing all the nocturnal animals. Clumps of snow fell from the bare tree branches. He slowed in front of the little cabin where he had grown up. Where he had hoped to create a new life.

Nostalgia hollowed out his gut. He'd do anything to crawl back into bed next to his wife. To settle into her warm embrace. To smell her floral shampoo. To feel her soft curves.

But he wasn't even sure she'd welcome him now. A distance had grown between them. One he wasn't sure they'd ever close.

Man, I've been stupid, stupid, stupid.

Determination steeled his spine. He'd figure out a way out of this. He'd gotten out of worse situations, hadn't he? He'd make it up to her. Tessa deserved the world.

Lights flickered in the woods. Panic slicked his cool skin. The headlights of snowmobiles were bearing down on him. He had to make sure they didn't barge into his house. Hurt his beautiful, innocent wife.

Jeb pulled back the throttle, making a big loop in the front yard. The freshly fallen snow sprayed in a fan as his back end fishtailed. He had to make sure they saw him, then he'd make a beeline for the woods. He had home-court advantage. He was intimate with every inch of this property. Maybe he'd lose them.

Icy wind and merciless low branches assaulted him as he maneuvered around the trees, following the same path he and his big brother had on their dirt bikes. The solid tree trunks and hidden roots made it treacherous, but once he got to the creek a half mile away, he could follow the trail that ran alongside it to the bridge. Then he could make it into town. Find someplace to hide. Maybe he'd go to Eddie's. Tell him what he'd done. Plead forgiveness. He'd be mad, but he'd help him. They were the closest thing to brothers.

Jeb risked a glance over his shoulder and the headlights of the snowmobiles bore down on him. "Yeah, you jerks. Follow me! Follow me." He pressed the thumb throttle and his sled picked up speed. He hoped the guys behind him would misjudge a large root or tree trunk, ending their pursuit. Adrenaline surged through his veins as an arctic blast caught a patch of exposed neck above his ski jacket. The clearing alongside the creek was ahead. He chanced another look over his shoulder.

"No, no, no…" At least one of the guys had gained on him.

Jeb accelerated, faster than prudent, but he had no choice. The back end of his sled slid out from behind him, causing him to fishtail. He cut a quick glance to the frozen creek. The headlight from one of his pursuers cut across his line of vision as he turned. He weighed his options.

Split-second decisions.

He'd never outrun them on a straight path. He needed to ramp up his advantage. If he made it across the frozen creek, he'd have another chance to lose them in the woods on the other side. Ditch his snowmobile, if necessary. Slip through the dense underbrush, wait them out, then hike into town.

The sled behind him rammed into him. *Now or never!*

Jeb cut a sharp right and made his way across the untouched snow covering the frozen creek. His speed and the fact that he had guys on his tail made it impossible to cut straight across. He had to take it at an angle, forcing him to be on the ice-covered creek for longer than he was comfortable. His momma had always told him and his brother to stay off the ice when they played in these same woods as kids. She warned them over and over that if they fell through the ice, their boots and heavy clothes would pull them under. Her detailed descriptions of a watery grave had kept him and Sawyer honest—and safe (as far as this creek).

His mother was dead. He wasn't a little boy anymore. And he was out of options.

The snow swirled, causing a dizzying effect. Focus on the opposite shore. *Focus.* Last thing he wanted to do was ride along the frozen creek on a quarter-ton machine. Not for any longer than he absolutely had to.

Jeb glanced toward the safety of the shore he had left. The men who had been following stayed along the path. Perhaps they had lost their nerve. A burst of hope had Jeb believing he might actually get out of this mess.

Thirty feet.

Twenty.

Come on. Come on. Come on.

He snuck another look toward the opposite shore and caught a glimpse of a stationary headlight.

Almost there.

A shifting under him spiked his heart rate. His snowmobile jolted up, hitting the hard edge of ice, the skis dipping under. His chest slammed against the handlebars. The cold water swirled around him. He flailed but couldn't get out from under the massive weight of the snowmobile. The memory of his momma's warning whispered across his brain. *You were right, Momma.*

Blackness threatened to consume him when, with one last jerk, he broke free from the weight of the sled. He pushed through the same opening in the ice and gulped in a glorious lungful of icy air. His numb, gloved hands pawed at the ice ledge. He heaved his chest up and kicked his cement boots.

I didn't come this far to only come this far.

He wanted to cry at his stupidity.

A light crossed his line of vision. He lifted his head, his teeth chattering. Someone climbed off the snowmobile on the shore only twenty or so feet away. Safety.

He lifted a hand to wave and his body slipped back a fraction. "Whoa." He dug in his elbows to pull himself farther out of the dark water. "Help! Help!"

Jeb King had no idea if the man he was yelling to was friend or foe, but the only thing he knew for sure was that he'd die if he didn't get out of this water.

He'd have to take his chances.

Something he had taken far too many of lately.

CHAPTER 2

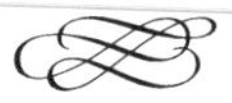

Tessa rolled over and tugged the quilt to cover her shoulder. The soft early morning light filtered in around the edges of the poorly fitting plastic blinds. She stretched out her foot to find her husband's spot cold. Then slowly the memory of him kissing her goodbye in the middle of the night floated to mind. That, and her feelings of frustration that he insisted on doing all these extra jobs because he thought she needed "stuff."

She snuggled into her pillow, not eager to get up. Their little cabin was drafty, but it was all theirs. Why did Jeb think she needed more? She never gave him any indication that she wasn't content.

After a moment, she opened one eye and checked the time. It was seven thirty in the morning and Jeb wasn't back. *Strange.* She let out a long breath and tried to quiet her mind. Jeb had been running a lot of errands recently, but this was the first one in the middle of the night. She tried to be a good wife and not pester him, but she didn't understand why he felt the need to work so hard. He already had a good job at the factory in town. Her questions angered him, and deep down she wondered if perhaps she had married him too quickly before getting to know him. *Really* know him.

Jeb King had been her chance to leave the Amish. Lately, she felt like maybe she had—like her *mammy* used to say—jumped out of the frying pan into the fire. Grandma was rarely wrong. She and Jeb had grown distant. He was quick to anger and moody. And Tessa struggled to reach him.

However, her Amish upbringing wouldn't allow her to leave him, even though her family hadn't approved of this marriage to begin with. She did value marriage. She had to make this work.

Her depressing thoughts crowded in on her, promising to bring her to tears. She had shed enough tears over the past few months in the darkness. Maybe she should get up, get dressed and make breakfast for Jeb. Then she remembered he'd promised to bring home breakfast sandwiches from the diner. She closed her eyes, deciding she'd give herself ten more minutes before she forced herself to face the day. She must have drifted back to sleep when she heard the squeak of snow under tires followed by heavy footsteps on her front porch.

She threw the covers back and swung out her legs. Panic pulsed through her veins, sending goose bumps across her already chilled skin. Jeb had taken the snowmobile because his vehicle couldn't navigate the deep snow up to the cabin. She grabbed her pink fuzzy robe off the hook and stuffed her arms into it. As she was tying the belt around her middle, someone pounded on the door.

"Sheriff's department. Mrs. King!" More pounding.

Tessa raced to the front door. *The sheriff's department?* She had one of those out-of-body experiences where she sensed she was standing at a pivotal moment in her life. *The before.* She feared *the after* with every ounce of her being.

Please let Jeb be okay. Please let him be okay, she repeated in her head, much as she had growing up when she wanted something with her whole heart. But until today, she hadn't wanted anything as much as she wanted her husband to be home safely.

Clutching the lapels of her robe, she drew the lacy curtain back. An SUV with the Hunters Ridge Sheriff's Department logo on the door sat outside. Somehow they had navigated her unplowed lane. She swallowed around a lump in her throat. She dropped the curtain and raced toward the door, each step feeling like she was plodding through quicksand.

Tessa undid the lock with trembling fingers and yanked open the door. Under normal circumstances, she would have yelped when the arctic wind hit her bare legs. Today, the biting cold barely registered. *"Yah?"* She had always been careful to hide her Amish roots, but in this moment she couldn't pretend to be anything other than what she was: a terrified wife. "Is it my husband?"

"Tessa King?" the deputy asked, ignoring her question.

Tessa nodded. *"Yah."*

"Is your husband here?" she asked.

"Um, no." Tessa looked around, as if he might have somehow returned home when she wasn't looking. A shudder racked her body.

The deputy held out her hand, not to shake hers, but rather indicating inside the cabin. "I'm Deputy Caitlin Flagler. Perhaps we can go inside where it's warm."

Tessa nodded and stepped back into the cabin. The fire had burned out sometime in the middle of the night and she hadn't yet had a chance to get it going again. "Can I get you some coffee?" she asked, her manners on autopilot as she pulled out a chair at the kitchen table and sat down. She had no intention of making coffee. The deputy did the same, but Tessa could see how her guest was taking in every inch of the cabin. What was she looking for?

"No coffee, thank you." The deputy folded her hands and placed them on the table. "I'll get right to it. A man walking his dog early this morning found a snowmobile registered to a Jebediah King at this address."

The deputy's keen gaze made Tessa's nerves hum. "He had to work last night. Sometimes it's easier to take the snowmobile into town. Did he park it someplace he wasn't supposed to? I'm sure he can explain." She pressed her fingers to her temple, feeling the dull start of a raging headache. Surely, the deputy wasn't paying her a visit over a parking ticket.

"Are you here alone?" the deputy asked. Tessa had never talked to a deputy before, and she knew the local department only had a few women. Somewhere deep in the part of her brain that was still thinking logically she wondered if they had intentionally sent a woman to talk to her. Less threatening and all.

Tessa nodded. A wave of nausea hit her hard and she breathed in through her nose, trying to quell the urge to empty the contents of her stomach. "I live here with my husband." But the deputy already knew that.

The deputy shook her head, a hint of red hair poking out from under her winter cap. "I mean, is there someone you can call so you're not alone now?"

Tessa laced her fingers and twisted her hands. "Please, you're scaring me." She swallowed around a knot of emotion in her throat. "What happened?"

"We're trying to put the pieces together." The deputy met her gaze and held it. "The snowmobile was partially submerged in the creek."

Tessa ran a shaky hand across her forehead. She stood and raced across the room to check the answering machine. They kept a landline due to the spotty cell reception out here deep in the woods. As former Amish, she hadn't yet seen the attraction of a mobile phone, especially since Jeb's attachment to his had been another issue in their new marriage. A message indicator flashed. Her heart rate spiked. She hadn't noticed it before. "There's a message." Hope blossomed in her belly.

Please, please, please let it be him.

With a shaky hand, she pressed the play button and her heart sank. The voice of an automated robocaller filled the space. Tessa immediately hit erase, annoyed at the machine for messing with her emotions. She turned around and found the deputy studying her. "Do you think my husband drowned?" Her voice cracked over the last word.

"Let's not jump to conclusions." The deputy leaned back and folded her arms over her chest. She had an odd bulk that suggested she must be wearing something under her uniform shirt. Her gaze raked across Tessa, probably trying to figure her out.

Tessa was used to that look. Many people didn't know how to deal with the Amish, and even though Tessa no longer followed the *Ordnung* and was now an outsider to her own family, she still undoubtedly gave off a timid Amish vibe. Or maybe Tessa thought far too much about every little thing, driving herself up the wall.

"It seems like a logical leap," Tessa said, mustering a spark of anger that surprised her. She didn't need to be shielded. She needed the truth. "Please tell me what's going on."

"That's what I'm trying to figure out." The deputy tucked a stray strand of red hair behind her ear. "Can you tell me where your husband works?"

"At the cheese factory. And...he...well, has some side jobs."

"Side jobs?" That last comment obviously piqued the deputy's interest and Tessa suddenly felt like she had broken a confidence.

"Deliveries. For one of his friends." Then before the

deputy could ask, Tessa added, "His name is Eddie. He lives in town."

"Do you know Eddie's last name?"

Tessa closed her eyes briefly, struggling to remember. They had hung out socially with Eddie and his girlfriend a few times, but she didn't know him that well. "I don't..." Something niggled at her brain. "Wait, it's Ward. Eddie Ward." She recalled Jeb mentioning it. Tessa pulled her robe sleeves down over her hands and tucked them under her armpits.

"Please, sit down," Deputy Flagler said, her tone annoyingly calm.

"If he's missing, we need to look for him," Tessa said, even as she complied and lowered herself so that she was perching on the edge of the kitchen chair.

"We have deputies searching and we've called in a dive team."

The colors in their cozy cabin turned monotone and her face went numb. "A dive team." She had trouble breathing. "You *do* think he drowned." She focused intently on the deputy's face, afraid her world was going to go black. She felt sick again. So, so sick.

"We need to check."

Tessa had an unreasonable urge to slap the sympathy off the deputy's face. "Why would he go on the frozen creek? It's obviously not safe." Her face tingled as she fought the tears.

"I'm sorry." The deputy smiled tightly. "Can I call someone for you?"

Tessa shook her head. She had no one. No one except her husband. That was what happened after she left her Amish family to marry an outsider. Her world had narrowed down to exactly one person.

The deputy stood. "I have to go. Do you have a cell phone so I can reach you?"

"A landline." She recited the number by rote.

The deputy walked toward the door, then turned to look at her. There was hesitation in her eyes. "I hate to ask this right now, but was your husband involved with the preppers' compound on the ridge? The one that was broken up a few weeks back?"

Tessa remembered hearing about some people getting arrested for transporting drugs across the US-Canadian border. They lived as if they expected the world to end. Maybe for them, it had. She shook her head slowly ignoring a whisper of a memory. "No, he wasn't."

Not that I'm aware of, anyway.

A wave of nausea hit her so hard she had to scramble away from the table. She barely made it to the toilet where she emptied what little contents were in her stomach.

After Tessa was finished, she sat back on her heels and cried.

CHAPTER 3

Five months later

Tessa's husband never came home that night, or any night after. Divers searched the creek, and volunteers from search and rescue combed the woods, worried that he had gotten himself out of the frigid water only to succumb to the elements. The only sign that Jeb had been out that fateful night was his snowmobile partially submerged in the water, and sled tracks and footprints on both sides of the creek. Following them didn't turn up anything.

Jeb King had simply vanished.

As much as Tessa didn't want Jeb to turn up dead, the not knowing was a special kind of misery. As it was, she woke up every morning wondering if this was going to be the day her husband returned. When—*if*—he did ever return, what was she going to say or do about it? She had disrupted her whole life to be with him, and then had to undo all the damage once he was gone. Would Jeb truly be that cruel to willingly leave her? Despite the problems they were having before that night, she couldn't believe he'd abandon her. Deep in her heart, she suspected he was dead.

That didn't make her feel any better.

"We're leaving, Tessa!" Joanna called from the other side of the bedroom door, snapping her out of her melancholy thoughts. "Dat said the van is going to be here soon. Tess! We're leaving."

Tessa climbed out of bed, something she dreaded, knowing the entire day stretched in front of her with little to occupy her time. She drew in a deep breath of the familiar soft, sweet summer breeze of her childhood. "Hold your horses, I'm coming."

She opened the door and found her sixteen-year-old sister wearing her favorite pale blue dress. She always wore it when she thought she might run into a certain boy in town. Tessa stifled a smile, grateful to be reminded of a much simpler time, before her choices made life more complicated. A lot more complicated.

"You look pretty this morning," Tessa said.

Joanna's cheeks blossomed with color. "Don't forget, you promised you'd take care of Daisy while we're gone. She likes carrots before bed because she gets hungry."

Tessa tilted her head. "Now how do you know she gets hungry?"

Joanna huffed her frustration, the way she did when her big sister teased her. How easily they had fallen into a familiar routine after Tessa's return two weeks ago after she had exhausted other living arrangements after Jeb's disappearance. She refused to stay in that cabin alone.

Tessa playfully chucked her sister's arm. "*Yah,* I will take care of Daisy if you promise to pick up blueberry licorice sticks for me." Her family was going to an auction in central New York and planned to stay the night with family who were in another Amish district that was in communion with Hunters Ridge.

"I'll get blueberry and root beer flavor." Joanna lowered her voice. "I wish you were going with us."

"Another time," Tessa said vaguely. Part of the arrangement of her return to Hunters Ridge was that she keep a low profile. Her hand reflexively touched her midsection, her baby bump barely visible under her full Amish dress.

You need to seek forgiveness her father had warned her when she moved back as rumors about her life had swirled around the Amish community of Hunters Ridge. It seemed to Tessa that the God-fearing people thrived on gossip. Last winter, the residents had been wrapped up in the outsiders living on the "doomsday preppers" compound, and as soon as the head of it was arrested for trafficking drugs, they turned their attention to something else. Unfortunately, that had been the mysterious disappearance of her husband. Tessa had to leave town, especially because she didn't feel safe in that remote cabin alone. Thankfully, her cousin in Pennsylvania had twin babies and needed her help. However, when it became more obvious that Tessa was expecting, her cousin asked her to leave. It was just too scandalous.

Now, her family hoped if she stayed tucked away on the farm, their neighbors would let them be. Her father had insisted that once this baby was born, he or she would be given to her older brother and his wife to raise, allowing Tessa a fresh start. Her parents had delusions that she'd then be able to meet a nice Amish man, perhaps in another Amish community where people didn't know her.

Tessa had no means to live on her own, and her silence regarding the matter was taken as acceptance. She had no idea what the future would bring, and all she knew was that she had only a few months to figure it out. All while living under her parents' roof, her days filled with light-duty chores and nagging worries.

"Joanna," her mother called from the front door, "*Mach*! Your father's getting impatient."

"Go on now." Tessa followed her sister down the stairs. When they reached the front door, she said, "I'll make sure the horses are taken care of. Don't worry."

"Don't overdo it," her mother said as a whisper of a smile crossed her lips and disappeared. Silver streaked the hair visible around her bonnet. Her mother's easygoing disposition had been replaced by a buzz of concern, and Tessa felt fully responsible. And she was sorry, but she was truly in a difficult position: she was living among the Amish but married to an outsider who had up and disappeared on her. "Tessa?" Her mother tilted her head.

Tessa blinked a few times. "I'll be careful." Then to lighten the mood, she added, "Have a safe trip. I sent Joanna with a few dollars to buy some candy."

Her mother's mouth twitched with unspoken words. She smiled tightly, then turned and hustled to the waiting van. Her father had hired a driver to take them to the auction because a horse and buggy would have taken far too much time, especially now during farming season. They'd stay with family for the night and return sometime tomorrow.

Tessa watched her family leave from the doorway. Her father didn't so much as wave. She wished it didn't hurt, but once upon a time she had been a daddy's girl. The first daughter after five sons. They had a great relationship until she reached the teen years and got what he called "worldly ideas." As much as she wanted to please her father, she had desired a different life for herself more.

Shoving aside her rambling thoughts, Tessa went back inside. Her childhood home stood eerily silent. This was the first time she had been left home alone since she had moved back. She grabbed a large glass of fresh-squeezed orange juice and went outside to sit on one of the rocking chairs. Maybe she should grab her romance novel she had tucked away in the bottom of her wardrobe. Her father would never approve of such reading material. For him, reading anything other than the Bible was a waste of time. Guilt niggled at her for thinking poorly of him. He generously provided her shelter. She needed to live by the rules, even if she didn't like them. She tilted back her head and closed her eyes, trying to be still in the moment.

The distinct sound of a clip-clop-clip sounded on the country road. Her heart rate spiked when she realized they were slowing down to turn up their lane. She set the glass down next to her chair and found herself gripping the arms of the rocker, wondering if she could slip inside unnoticed before they reached the house. She had hesitated too long. A young Amish man lifted his arm in a friendly greeting.

Tessa waved in return, a sinking feeling settling in the pit of her stomach. She quickly adjusted the fabric around her waist and tried to ignore her buzzing nerves.

The young Amish man hopped off the wagon and strolled over to her. He looked vaguely familiar. It wasn't until he got closer that she recognized him as Camp Bontrager, the youngest of the five Bontrager boys who lived across town. He strongly resembled his older brothers who were closer to her age. She had overheard her parents saying they suspected Camp was sweet on their youngest daughter.

"Guder mariye." Camp called good morning with a wave. *"Wie bischt?" How are you?*

"Ich bin gut." I am well. Tessa plucked at her dress and felt the heat of his scrutiny.

"Is Joanna home? I'd like to invite her to go into town with me." He shuffled his feet. "I asked your father and he gave me permission."

"Joanna's not home. She won't be back until tomorrow. They went to the auction."

"Okay." The single word conveyed his defeat. Then he tilted his head. "Are you Tessa?"

"*Yah.* Can I help you?" She held her breath, hoping he would go away. She didn't need one of the Bontrager boys spreading gossip about her. They had a habit of pointing out others' faults, as if that somehow lifted them up.

"I'm surprised to see you here," he said, his tone oddly flat.

She arched an eyebrow but didn't say anything. Had the young man come here to confirm what he had heard in town under the pretense of visiting her sister? That the prodigal daughter had come back? The idea made her flush. Yet she wasn't naive. It wasn't often that a twenty-five-year-old Amish daughter returned home after her *Englisch* husband went missing. Of course there would be gossip, despite her parents' best efforts to have her stay hidden at home. This arrangement hadn't spared her from gossip, only from the stares and whispers.

"How come you didn't go with your family?" There was a strange tone in his voice, or maybe she was reading too much into it. She was familiar with the Bontrager family. They were what Jeb would call holier-than-thou, which said a lot for an Amish family. One of the boys was her age and he never participated in drinking, smoking, or goofing around. Yet he liked to be a witness to it. Years ago, he had made a point to tell her father that he had seen her at a bonfire acting inappropriately with *Englischers*. Tessa might have had a beer or two and flirted with some cute boys, but her actions were mostly harmless. Unless you were Amish, of course.

Her father had forbidden her to go out the next weekend. Funny that soon after, she'd met Jeb. At a bonfire. Their romance had burned fast and bright. Tessa married Jeb six months after meeting him and moved away for good. Or at least that had been the plan.

Refusing to let him get to her, she smiled and said, "I stayed home. That's all."

"Are you sick?" The smugness of his question rubbed her the wrong way.

"Excuse me?"

"Because you stayed home? I figured you mustn't be feeling *gut.*"

Tessa shrugged, searching her brain for a way to get rid of him without causing a scene. She tried an apathetic stare. It didn't work.

"Joanna said you've been sick."

Heat crawled up her neck. Her little sister must have heard her in the bathroom. She was still suffering from morning sickness. Did her sister know? Their parents had asked that Tessa hide her pregnancy for as long as possible. Their house. Their rules.

Tessa tried not to bristle and smiled tightly. "Perhaps some food poisoning. I'm fine." She stood and walked toward the door. "Now, if you'll excuse me, I have some chores to do."

"Good day," Camp said as he spun on his heels and strode back to his wagon.

Tessa slipped inside and pressed her back against the door, wondering if she'd ever *not* be the subject of gossip.

CHAPTER 4

A soft breeze blew in Tessa's bedroom window and she woke with a start. The room was cast in heavy shadows and it took a moment to reorient herself. She rolled over and the book she had been reading fell off her belly. She smiled. Ah, she had dozed off after reading all evening. An absolute luxury.

She had been able to shake the uneasy feelings from Camp Bontrager's unexpected visit and enjoyed the rest of the day. She had come by her distrust in men honestly. And Jeb's disappearance had totally messed with her, making her looks sideways at some poor Amish boy looking to court her sister. However, the Bontrager boys weren't exactly unknown to her.

A flash of lightning illuminated the room and a rumble of thunder sounded in the distance. "Daisy," she muttered to herself, sitting up quickly. She had promised her sister she'd give her horse her evening treat. She pressed her hand to her forehead, dizzy from sitting up too fast. She had also skipped dinner. *Not smart.* Her sister would never know if she kept her word or not, but she'd know. And she had made a promise.

She had changed into yoga pants and a T-shirt before lying down to read. She considered putting on her plain clothing, but then decided no one would see her anyway. Descending the staircase slowly, she rubbed the sleep from her eyes. In the kitchen, she grabbed a handful of carrots and a kerosene lamp.

As she headed across the field to the barn, the warm air whipped her hair back. Streaks of lightning zigzagged the night sky. It smelled like rain. Jeb used to laugh at her and tell her no one could smell rain. But she could, and she was never wrong. The rustling of the cornstalks unnerved her, reminding her of the last night she had spent in the cabin she had shared with Jeb. She had the distinct feeling someone had been there when she wasn't home. The cabin seemed in order, but off. Like someone had moved things and then put them back in *almost* the same place, but not quite. She hadn't been able to shake the uneasy feeling that she was being watched. But even after contacting the sheriff's department, nothing came of it. One deputy suggested her unease must be the result of the shock over her husband's disappearance.

But that was all months ago. In another location. She was home now.

You're being silly.

Quickening her pace, she tucked the carrots under her arm and peeled open the barn door. She wondered if she'd spend the rest of her life having flashbacks to her life with Jeb. She worried she'd never get over him until she had closure. She was left in limbo, surrounded by a swirling cloud of grief, anger and worry.

"Hey guys," Tessa said cheerily as she stepped into the barn. There were four stalls for the horses, two on either side of the barn. Her family owned two American Saddlebreds for pulling the buggy and two draft horses for farm equipment. Even though she had promised to spoil Daisy, one of the Saddlebreds, she had to give each of the horses a carrot, taking time to talk and stroke their manes. Her father had hired an Amish boy from nearby to feed the horses their regular meals.

With each horse visit, she felt her undefined anxiety dissolving. She smiled to herself. Maybe she had missed this place more than she had realized.

She was brushing Daisy when another rumble of thunder, this time louder, seemed to agitate the horse. "It's okay. It's okay," she said soothingly. "I'll stay with you. I'm not going anywhere."

The skies opened up and rain pelted the roof of the barn. Daisy huffed and neighed, unsettled by the storm.

"It's okay. It's okay," Tessa repeated over and over, a mantra she had often said to herself. "It'll all be okay."

Daisy settled in and Tessa stepped out of the stall. She grabbed a horse blanket and spread it out on the barn floor and sat down, leaning her back against the wall, waiting the storm out.

"I'm right here, Daisy. I'm right here."

Tessa wasn't sure how long she had been there when she heard a car close by. She pushed to her feet then shouts made her freeze in place. Daisy stilled, as if she sensed danger. Uncertain what to do, Tessa opened the stall door and slipped inside. Maybe whoever it was would go away.

Go away, go away.

The barn door creaked open. Shuffled footsteps. Glass shattering. A whoosh.

Flames!

Her pulse thrummed in her ears. She had to get out. Get the horses out!

Tessa opened the stall and Daisy reared up, terrified by

the heat and flames. Panic and smoke made Tessa's throat close. She patted Daisy and urged her. "Come on, girl. Come on." She fought to keep her tone calm, encouraging. "Go, girl. Go." She patted her and still the animal wouldn't budge.

Desperate, Tessa ran to the other stalls, setting the other horses free. Thankfully they ran out the back door to the fenced-in field with minimal prodding. Coughing and sputtering, she rushed back to Daisy.

"Come on, girl! Come on!" Smoke made her eyes tear and panic clouded her thinking. "Please, Daisy! We have to get out of here."

Then, as if guided by a need for self-preservation, Daisy bolted out of the stall, sending Tessa reeling backward, off-balance. She landed with an oomph and cried out in pain. Flames raced across the rafters.

She tried to scrabble across the floor. The structure groaned.

Something slammed into the back of her head. Instinctively, she lifted her hands and touched the tender spot. "Oh no..." she groaned. Stars danced in her line of vision. Feeling woozy, she stumbled toward the door, terror and heat licking at the back of her neck.

The siren wailed as the fire engine left the bay and cautiously turned onto Main Street. Sitting shotgun, Sawyer King gave the driver the all-clear to proceed. An Amish woman and her two young sons stopped on the sidewalk and watched the truck pass. Sawyer would never grow tired of the adrenaline rush from responding to a fire call. The station here was less busy than the one where he worked in California before he returned to Hunters Ridge after his brother Jeb's disappearance. But this had been the second barn fire in recent months. This evening's rain wouldn't put a dent in the long drought they'd been having.

A horse and buggy pulled over to the side of the road to let the fire engine pass. The houses and barns along all the back roads were familiar to him. When he was a teen, he ran wild with his classmates and the Amish during their *Rumspringa.* Looking back, it was an odd mix of kids, but growing up *Englisch* among the Amish hadn't seemed strange to him. It was just how it was.

Sawyer had been back in town for months, but memories kept slamming into him when he recognized an old haunt where they had late-night bonfires, drinking games in someone's barn, and fields where pickup trucks and buggies parked side by side.

When the fire engine got closer, a black plume of smoke billowed into the air above a thick row of trees. "Looks like it might be fully engulfed." His pulse quickened and the familiar surge of adrenaline had him in go-mode. As soon as the engine stopped, it would be all hands on deck.

The driver pressed closer to the large steering wheel and angled his head closer to the windshield. "Sure does." He turned up the lane and the extent of the fire came into view. Something about this location niggled at Sawyer's brain, but he didn't have time to process it.

His captain hopped out of the truck and gave commands. One of the firefighters went to the house and pounded on the door to account for any residents. No one answered.

"Who called it in?" Sawyer asked as he unraveled the hose from the pumper truck.

"Neighbor."

Sawyer glanced over his shoulder, then handed the hose to a junior firefighter. "I'll check for animals in the barn."

In full gear, Sawyer jogged to the barn. He walked around the side and found a woman unconscious on the ground, just outside the barn. His eyes rose to the flames shooting out of the structure, ten feet from where she lay. He had to get her away from the structure before it collapsed. Panting behind his mask, he bent down into the heavy smoke and picked her up. Her head lolled back and her hair flowed behind her. Focusing on getting her to safety, he strode toward the fire engines and laid her on the ground. He checked her airway and she turned her head and coughed violently. He peeled back his mask, cleared his vision, and that was when he recognized her.

Tessa. He thought she had left town after his brother disappeared.

"You're okay," he said reassuringly as she blinked repeatedly. "Is anyone else in the barn?"

"No." Her eyes were wide yet she seemed to struggle to take things in. "My family..." She coughed. "They won't be home till tomorrow."

"Animals?" he asked.

"All out." She coughed again, seeming to struggle to catch a breath.

Then he hollered to his crew. "Where's the bus?"

"Five minutes out."

A steady stream of water flowed from the pumper truck to the fire. Thankfully the barn fire was contained in a short amount of time.

Tessa seemed agitated and tried to wave off the paramedics when they arrived. He stepped back, allowing them to do their work.

"Name?" the paramedic asked.

"Tessa. Tessa Sutter." She coughed again until tears streaked the soot on her face.

She was going by her maiden name. Did she think her husband—his brother—was dead?

"Is there anyone we can call?" the paramedic asked.

She shook her head again. "Can someone see that the horses are okay?" Her voice sounded raspy. "They should be secure in the back field. Can someone check?" She lifted her arm and held it out. Just then a flash brightened the scene. Sawyer turned to see a photographer.

"Back off," Sawyer said, holding up his hand to the interloper, feeling protective of Tessa when he had no business feeling that way.

"I'm with the local newspaper." The photographer took a step back.

"Then you should know the Amish don't like their photo taken." Sawyer glared at him.

The young man frowned and jerked his chin in Tessa's direction. "She's Amish? Could have fooled me." He shrugged, probably indicating her casual *Englisch* clothing. With a smug smile, he turned around and sauntered off, satisfied that he had gotten a photo of the victim that was worthy of publication.

Sawyer recalled discovering a photo of himself in a California newspaper once, his face covered in soot and etched with exhaustion. The human element, a friend had told him, sold more papers than a forest fire. People had hounded him for months to tell his story. How he had ended up working for days on end battling relentless fires. But Sawyer didn't want the publicity. He just wanted to do his job.

The paramedics helped Tessa onto the gurney, then into the ambulance. Any thoughts about telling her who he was vanished the minute the doors slammed shut. He turned on his heel and his gaze fell on the firefighters spraying water on the embers.

His captain strolled over to him. "I want you to stick around and help me with the investigation."

"Any chance the fire is weather related? There were some lightning strikes in the area," Sawyer said, mostly just shooting the breeze. It would be his job to find evidence, not speculate.

"This is the second barn fire in the past two months," the captain said. "The one at the Schwartz farm was ruled accidental. The elderly gentleman said he tipped over a kerosene lamp. The dried hay and wood made it a tinderbox. But that family was pretty tight-lipped overall. Refused to let us investigate."

"That's how it usually is with the Amish," Sawyer said. Growing up in Hunters Ridge, he was familiar with their ways. And his parents—former Amish—shared a lot about their upbringing. Mostly that they despised it.

"Maybe this was more of the same. Despite the recent storm, we haven't had much rain." His captain pointed to the glowing embers. "Do some digging here, then I suppose we'll have a deputy follow up with the victim. Maybe this one will be more willing to talk."

"Mind if I go up to the hospital myself? I know Tessa."

"Oh yeah?" The captain raised his eyebrows.

"She's my sister-in-law."

His boss narrowed his gaze. "I thought this was an Amish residence. One of the neighbors said as much."

"Long story. Mind if I explain it another time?"

"Sure. If you think she'll talk to you, by all means go now."

"I don't know if she will, but I'd like to try. She was married to my brother who disappeared back in February."

"She's had a tough go of it." The captain took off his helmet and his hair stood up in sweaty tufts. "That was a tough thing, about your brother. Still no word?"

"No word. That's why I'd like to talk to Tessa. Last I heard she was out of town. Now that she's back, maybe she's willing to talk."

"You don't think this blaze is somehow connected to her husband's disappearance?" He tucked his helmet under his arm and scrubbed his hand over his face. "I imagine it's a stretch, but worth checking out. We'll bring the sheriff's department in on this."

"Let me walk the scene while it's fresh." Sawyer turned and slowly strolled the perimeter. He studied the structure for clues. Not too far from where he had found Tessa, he discovered broken glass. Perhaps another kerosene lamp? He pulled out his phone and took a few photos.

He rolled back on his heels and considered a few things. Tessa was married to his brother. His brother was missing. He twisted his lips, thinking. The barn fire here might be similar to another Amish barn fire. Was there a tie there? Was Tessa's family somehow connected to the Schwartz family? To find the answers, he'd have to start with Tessa.

CHAPTER 5

Tessa stared out the hospital window as the first fingers of pink and purple stretched across the early morning sky. The ceiling lights from her hospital room were reflected in the glass. Her head was pounding and her heart hurt. *Please let the horses be okay.* It seemed her life was one tragic event after another. Maybe this was her punishment for leaving the Amish in the first place.

She let out a long breath and tried to relax. She had a hard time believing God operated that way. After last night, she should be exhausted, but she couldn't shut off her brain. Snippets of the fire, of Daisy bolting, her falling. Her rescue. Something about the man who carried her away from the barn seemed familiar. From a dream? She couldn't quite grasp what she was trying to remember and it frustrated her. All this stress wasn't good for her. Wasn't good for the baby. She ran her hand across her abdomen, truly grateful the baby was okay. The doctor assured her everything would be fine. *Focus on that.*

She closed her eyes and drifted off. A quiet knock on the

door jolted her awake. The bright sun outside her window suggested she must have dozed off for an hour or two.

She turned her head on the pillow, fully expecting a hospital employee with her breakfast. Instead, she found someone she hadn't seen in years. Heat inexplicably flushed her face. His hair was shorter than she remembered, he had a few more lines on his face, but the warmth and kindness behind his eyes was a balm to her frayed nerves. Sawyer. Sawyer King.

"It was you," she breathed. "You rescued me from the fire yesterday." She blinked slowly, a few of the pieces snapping into place. "Yes, it was definitely you." His hair was still the same sandy brown from when he was a teenager, but the thick, scruffy locks had been cut. Shorter on the sides and longer on top, a stylish cut. It suited him.

"You did a pretty good job of rescuing yourself." He studied her with those same intense brown eyes that seemed to regard her like he had when she first started dating Jeb. She had always been afraid to read too much into it.

Had he thought she wasn't good enough for his little brother? Sawyer had always seemed distant, hard to read. She blinked, trying not to be self-conscious about this handsome man standing at the foot of her hospital bed.

Sawyer's here. She struggled to wrap her head around the turn of events.

"I found you outside the building," he said, interrupting her rambling thoughts. "Do you remember what happened?"

She pushed up on one elbow and winced, then laid back down. She grabbed the remote and elevated the head of her bed. She smiled, feeling self-conscious in her hospital gown. "My head is pounding," she said, not answering his question. What had happened?

"Are you okay?" he asked, taking a step closer.

"I'll be fine." She sniffed. "I remember going to check on

the horses at night. A thunderstorm was brewing so I decided to stay in the barn until it passed. Daisy seemed skittish." Tessa rubbed her forehead, struggling to pick out the details from her hazy memory. "I heard a car and something crash. Glass, I think. And wow, the fire spread quickly. Do you think someone set it?" Uttering the words out loud made a fresh wave of panic prickle her skin. She had been feeling uneasy yesterday.

"That's what I'm trying to find out. I'm a fire investigator with the Hunters Ridge fire department."

Fire investigator?

"You look pale," he said. Just what any girl wanted to hear. "Are you sure you're okay?"

"I will be when they let me go home," Tessa said. "And when you figure out how the fire started."

"Any ideas? Has your family had any run-ins with anyone?" Sawyer asked.

She shook her head adamantly, but that was a lie. She had a million ideas, but none she wanted to share. And none that had to do with her family. She cleared her throat and decided to mention the elephant in the room. "Jeb told me you were a firefighter. I thought you lived in California."

Sawyer nodded. "I did. I moved back. After Jeb."

Tessa self-consciously gathered the blanket around her midsection. "I didn't know you were in town. I only moved back to Hunters Ridge myself recently." She scratched her hand. "Are you staying for good?" she asked because she didn't have the emotional capacity to discuss Jeb with his big brother.

"I'll probably leave after I get everything settled here."

"Everything settled?" She fingered the edge of the rough hospital blanket. Unease wormed its way up her spine. She didn't have any answers for him. She didn't have any answers for herself.

"The cabin needs to be sorted. I'll sell the land." He shrugged. "Who knows where the wind will take me after that."

Of course, the house she and Jeb had shared. It had been Jeb and Sawyer's childhood home. "I'm sorry about Jeb."

"Yeah, me too." Sawyer's lips quirked. He looked like he wanted to say more but didn't.

"Don't believe all the rumors," Tessa said, suddenly feeling like she had to defend her husband, maybe even herself. "He was a good man." She turned her face away from him and swiped at a tear. She had such conflicted feelings about her missing husband, and his handsome brother brought them all flooding to the surface.

The silence stretched between them for a beat too long. There was an electrical undercurrent in the air that made her uneasy. Sawyer was always the more reserved of the brothers. The one with a plan. The less impulsive of the pair. He was holding back. He wasn't going to bombard her with questions while she lay in a hospital bed after nearly getting trapped in a barn fire. But she needed to know what he was thinking. Did he blame her? Did he know something that he was afraid to tell her?

"Has someone contacted your family to let them know you're here?" he asked, sending her mind reeling in another direction. "I heard they were away for the weekend."

She tilted her head back, exposing her delicate neck, and laughed, a mirthless sound. "No phones, remember?"

"Sounds like an excuse. There's a way to track them down. You said they went to an auction."

"Near Syracuse." She reached out but stopped short of touching his hand. "I don't want them to cut their trip short. There's nothing they can do, and I don't…" She let the words trail off, aware that complaining about her mother's tendency to hover would be disrespectful. "I'll be fine and home before they are."

"You said you heard a car and a smashing sound before the fire. Anything else?"

Tessa ran her hand slowly over her forehead. "No. It all happened so fast. Does..." She glanced toward the door. "Do you think this has to do with Jeb's disappearance?"

Sawyer dipped his chin, clearly caught off guard by the question. "I don't have any reason to believe that." He paused and narrowed his gaze. "Do you?"

Her lower lip quivered. "There're so many unanswered questions surrounding her husband's disappearance."

"There was definitely evidence of arson. Someone threw what appears to be a Molotov cocktail—a bottle with an accelerant and rags—into the building."

A wave of fear made Tessa feel nauseous. The nurse said that was to be expected with a concussion. "Any ideas who did it?"

"Not yet. But I'd like to help you and the sheriff's department find some answers."

Part of her was afraid to dig too deep. Could she handle finally finding the truth?

"One of the nurses stopped me on the way in," Sawyer said, interrupting her thoughts. "You'll be able to go home this morning. I'd be happy to drive you. That's the first order of business." She appreciated that he was trying to lighten the mood.

"You should have led with that news. Yes, I would appreciate a ride. Thank you." She didn't have much choice. Her head hurt too much to call for a ride and then deal with the inevitable mundane chitchat while being held hostage in the back seat.

"Can I ask you one more thing?" Sawyer asked.

"Yeah."

"Have you heard anything about the fire at the Schwartzes' last month?"

Another barn fire. Tessa frowned. "That happened while I was living in Pennsylvania. I heard Old Man Schwartz dropped a lamp."

"Do you think that's likely?"

"He's elderly. Maybe." Tessa was careful to keep her answer simple, feeling ever bit of Sawyer's scrutiny. His eyes had a way of reading a person's soul. Or maybe just hers.

The sound of rubber soles squeaking on the tile made Tessa glance toward the door. A nurse scooted into the room and pushed back the curtain. "You ready to blow this pop stand?"

Tessa nodded. She wanted to leave the hospital, but she wasn't ready to face her parents. She had already complicated their lives before the fire.

"Do you have a ride?" the nurse asked.

"I'm taking her," Sawyer said, a lightness to his face that she wanted to bottle.

The nurse looked at her for confirmation.

Tessa blinked a few times. "You're not offering me a ride on your motorcycle, are you?"

Sawyer shook his head. "I left my bike in Cali. I have a truck now."

"Why don't you get it and pull it around front," the nurse said. "I'll bring Tessa down in a wheelchair, per hospital policy."

"Okay." Sawyer gave her a warm smile that made her miss Jeb. The Jeb she thought she knew.

Tessa watched Sawyer walk out of her room, then the nurse leaned in and whispered conspiratorially, "Your husband and you are going to have a gorgeous baby?"

"Oh, no he's—"

Before she had a chance to finish, the nurse said, "He's

very handsome." She waggled her eyebrows for effect. "I'd hang on to him."

"He's..." Tessa didn't bother to finish what she had been about to say. She smoothed her hands over her belly and immediately felt like she had done something wrong. She was married to Jeb.

CHAPTER 6

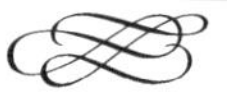

Sawyer pulled up to the front hospital entrance and got out to help Tessa into his truck. She had a small white bandage on her forehead and her hair was twisted up into a neat bun. She was wearing blue hospital scrubs since apparently no one had been able to bring her clean clothes. She looked far different than the free-spirited woman he and his brother had hung out with during her *Rumspringa* years. Sawyer had a keen memory of her long brown hair blowing behind her while she held tight around Jeb's waist on his motorcycle. He had been jealous of his brother.

Back then, Sawyer and Jeb had been planning to leave Hunters Ridge. Ride their motorcycles across the country. Just the two of them.

Until Tessa came into their lives.

Sawyer suspected his brother was growing cool on the idea of leaving Hunters Ridge and Tessa had been an excuse. However, if given the option, Sawyer would have given up his plans for a woman like her. But no one asked him.

Tessa muttered something as she fished for the seat belt.

"Pretty soon I won't be able to get this across me." She laughed, but it didn't sound joyful.

Sawyer's gaze snapped to her abdomen and for the first time he realized something he had been too oblivious to notice. "You're pregnant?" The words came out in an air of disbelief and he didn't want to explore the jab of something akin to jealousy. Still.

This time Tessa genuinely laughed. "You carried me away from the fire. I feel like I'm as big as a house. You didn't notice?"

Sawyer shook his head slowly and dragged a hand through his hair. "Jeb's?"

At the mention of her husband, Tessa's face turned a crimson red. "Of course it's my husband's." She sounded both offended and embarrassed at the same time.

"I'm sorry. I didn't mean it the way it sounded." Sawyer was recalibrating a million thoughts swirling through his head. His brother was going to be a father. Then another thought slammed into him. "Did Jeb know?"

Tessa turned away and stared out the window. "No. I only realized I was pregnant after he disappeared. He had no idea. You can imagine my shock when I was dealing with his accident and then…" She patted her belly.

"And everything is okay with the baby? I mean, after the fire."

Tessa nodded. "Everything's fine. Thank goodness." She turned to face him. "Do you know if my parents are back from the auction?"

"I don't know. Your neighbors called me to tell me they're taking care of the horses."

"Good." Tessa threaded her fingers and twisted her hands.

Sawyer pulled out of the hospital parking lot. "Do you need anything before I take you home?"

"No." She inhaled deeply, then exhaled. "Thank you."

"When are you due?" Sawyer asked, still trying to wrap his head around this recent news.

"October." She ran her palm across her belly. "Sometimes I wonder if things would have been different if we had found out a week earlier that I was pregnant."

"How?"

She bit her lip and seemed to give it some consideration. "Maybe I could have convinced him to stay home that night. If he knew there was a baby on the way."

Sawyer and Tessa hadn't had a chance to discuss what she thought had happened to his brother. "Do you know where he was going?" He wished he wasn't driving so he could watch her reaction. Sometimes it was the little tells, the lip twitches, the look in the eyes that spoke louder than any words.

"Another job for Eddie Ward. We fought a lot about them. He was always gone. He thought we needed the money. Yet I had everything I needed." Tessa shrugged. "The sheriff's department claims Eddie didn't have a job for Jeb that night." She sighed heavily, as if she had been over this a million times. She probably had. "Jeb might have been lying. Maybe Eddie was. I don't know what to believe. Jeb and I hadn't been getting along. That haunts me, you know."

Her admission caught him off guard. His brother and Tessa hadn't been getting along?

"Maybe knowing this baby was coming would have made everything better," she added, not sounding very convinced.

Sawyer wasn't so sure but kept his thoughts to himself.

"I can't believe he'd leave me, but the alternative is worse."

Sawyer feared the worst, too, but admitting that would do nothing for Tessa. It would be best if he waited until he had time to do more digging. "I talked to his friend, Eddie. I knew him from growing up here. He was always a trouble-maker as a kid, but he and Jeb were tight. He told me the same thing, that he didn't have a job for Jeb that night." Eddie claimed he was as baffled as anyone else that Jeb would take his snowmobile out across the icy creek. Any kid growing up around here who roamed the woods knew to stay off the frozen creek.

"I never understood why Jeb did a lot of what he did. I suspect it was mostly for money." Tessa sighed. "He had a stable job at the cheese factory."

When Sawyer had heard his brother worked at the factory in town, it threw him for a loop. As a kid, Jeb vowed he'd never work there. Said he'd rob a bank first. Both boys grew up associating the factory with their dad's foul moods. Their dad would leave the factory, go drinking, then come home and take out all his anger on them. Any memory of his father brought up feelings he'd rather forget. He cleared his throat. "Do you know anything about his late-night jobs?"

She shook her head. "Not really. There was regret in that single statement. "Deliveries to local companies, but never in the middle of the night. Late, sure, but never a text rousing him out of bed."

Sawyer made a mental note to talk to Eddie again. Press him. Sawyer wouldn't put it past the guy to lie. Maybe he had something to hide.

Sawyer checked his sideview mirror and pulled out around a slow-moving Amish buggy. When they arrived at Tessa's house, the acrid smell reached his nose. The fire had reduced the barn to a pile of smoldering timber, with only a side and a back wall still partially standing. As a firefighter, it was an all-too familiar smell. The forest fires in California had been relentless. Beating them back had been a full-time job for months.

He parked in front of the house. "Let me help you inside."

She looked like she wanted to say no, but she didn't. He was grateful, too, because her coloring was off and he needed to make sure she was okay. He hopped out and walked around to her side of the truck.

"I should have picked up some food for you," he said, his hand hovering near her elbow.

She waved at him in dismissal. "There's food inside. I'll be fine."

She paused at the front door of the house. She reached out and turned the handle. It swung open.

"I'm sorry," Sawyer said. "I should have made sure the house was secure yesterday when they took you to the hospital."

"We never lock the house." She turned to face him, an unspoken goodbye on her lips. "My *mem* and *dat* should be home soon."

Sawyer held out his hand to the two rockers on the porch. "Can we sit? Chat? Not long, I promise."

Her eyebrows quirked. "I'm tired, Sawyer."

"Please, it's important."

Tessa nodded.

"Can I get you some water first?

She nodded again. Sawyer slipped inside the shadowy house and got her a glass of water from the tap. The smell from the fire had gotten trapped inside, but he decided it wasn't his place to air out the house. As she said, her family would be home soon. When he returned, he found her sitting on a rocker she had dragged into the shade.

"Thank you," she said, accepting the drink.

Sawyer sat down and rested his forearms on his thighs. "I loved...love," he quickly corrected himself to the present tense, "Jeb, but he could be impulsive."

Tessa took another sip of water and averted her gaze. "Like marrying me?" A shy smile tipped the corners of her mouth.

"No, I consider that to be one of his better decisions."

Pink crept up her neck and cheeks and he immediately regretted making her feel uncomfortable. "I was talking about other decisions."

Tessa seemed pensive, perhaps waiting for him to continue.

"Do you know if Jeb was involved with that compound that was dismantled over the winter? I've done some digging—"

Tessa's eyes grew watery. "No, absolutely not. Why would you ask? That group was into drugs. Your brother hated when anyone was under the influence. After dealing with your father."

"Perhaps he thought it would be a way to make some quick money. I can't imagine he liked working at the factory."

A tear trailed down her cheek and she quickly wiped it away. "He'd never get involved with something like that. Never." Her shoulders squared and her chin jutted out, but something in her tone lacked conviction. "He was a good man."

Sawyer could sense the doubt he had planted, and he hated himself for that. Or maybe it was there all along, but the fire had left her vulnerable, unable to hide her true emotions.

Tessa set her glass down on the porch and clasped her elbows over her growing baby bump. "As much as I want him to come home, to be a father to this baby, I can't figure out why he'd stay away, unless he was...dead." Her voice cracked on the last word.

Or unless he was running from someone or something, but Sawyer cared too much for Tessa to push her on this point. She looked frail, shaky, and...lost. He needed to let it go. *For now.* But he hated the idea of her being here alone. Had someone been trying to kill her, or just scare her?

Perhaps they thought the barn was empty since her family was out of town. Sometimes arsonists were trying to make statements, and not necessarily looking to injure anyone.

"I'm tired," she said, pushing to her feet. "Thank you for bringing me home." She took a few steps toward the door and turned. "It was nice to see you again, Sawyer." She sounded sincere and nostalgic. Many times he had wondered *what if.*

"Nice to see you, too. Next time, let's do it under different circumstances." He smiled, trying to lighten the mood. Her gaze seemed to linger on him for a bit before she went inside.

Sawyer stared over the smoldering remains of the barn and worried Hunters Ridge had a serial arsonist on its hands. He'd have to work with the sheriff's department to find the perpetrator. And somehow, he'd have to find a way to protect his brother's wife and his unborn niece or nephew.

CHAPTER 7

The tears fell as soon as Tessa closed the door. She pressed her body against the cool wood and wondered if her hormones were making her so darned moody. She had forgotten the kindness in Sawyer's eyes. He had been the gentler of the two brothers, and for whatever reason she had pursued the wilder one, perhaps because Jeb was willing to throw caution to the wind and marry her and take her away from her Amish roots.

Tessa scoffed and swiped at the tears. "Look how that worked out for you," she muttered to herself. She levered off the door and scolded herself to pull it together. Her head throbbed from yesterday's concussion. The gross smell in here didn't help, neither would crying. Yet the thing making her head hurt the most were snippets of her conversation with Sawyer.

Someone had set the barn fire.

Had Jeb been involved with the preppers group?

Tessa had vehemently denied it. Almost on reflex. But would it be so crazy for Jeb to do something if he thought it would be easy money? He made deliveries. What if the deliveries involved something illegal? He did hate working in the factory, but...would he?

She couldn't shake the question: Had Jeb been involved with something that had put them both in danger? Something that had resulted in his disappearance.

Deep inside, anger flickered to life. Anger that had been simmering below the surface for months now, mingled with fear and sadness. A horrible combination that made her stomach ache. It wasn't good for the baby.

Her entire situation wasn't good for the baby.

Ultimately, she was angry because her husband had abandoned her. It was hard to acknowledge, but she hadn't trusted him—not fully—for a long time prior to his disappearance. She didn't like the crowd he was hanging with. She didn't like that he came home hours after his shift ended, leaving her to bide her time in the isolated cabin where his childhood memories seemed to haunt every aspect of their lives. And now she was mad at herself for all the poor choices she had made along the way, leaving her in a wretched position.

Alone.

Pregnant.

And ashamed.

The discovery of a surprise pregnancy the week after her husband disappeared added to her feelings of overwhelm. She'd had no idea how she'd provide for a child, and she didn't feel safe in the cabin in the middle of nowhere. She was convinced someone had been in her house. That someone was watching her. But she had no proof.

So it was only logical that she jump at the opportunity to help a dear cousin who had recently had twins. That situation worked well, until it didn't. When she feared she couldn't hide her pregnancy any longer, she came home to make a deal with the bishop. (It felt like the devil, sometimes.)

The memory of her father's hands curled into fists, ready to slug the bishop when he suggested she stay out of sight, was etched into her brain. She had, for the flicker of a moment, thought he was going to give him a piece of his mind. But now she understood better. The anger was directed toward her. While her mother remained silent, Tessa had agreed with the conditions which would allow her parents to hold their heads up high in the community.

Feeling queasy, Tessa went to the kitchen and got another glass of water. She stared out the window at the ruins of the barn. She put her free hand on her belly. "We'll figure this out, baby."

Despite wanting to climb into bed and pull the quilt over her head, Tessa got dressed in her plain clothes. She started cutting the vegetables for an evening stew for her family. She was grateful to occupy her mind with a mundane task.

Her distraction was interrupted by the sound of her father's voice outside. "It's a total loss," he said. "I wouldn't have believed it unless I saw it with my own eyes."

Tessa rushed to the window overlooking the yard.

"Where is Tessa?" The worry and strain were evident in her mother's voice.

Tessa rushed outside. "I'm here. I'm here."

Her mother's gaze swept over her. "Are you okay?"

Tessa nodded, lips trembling.

"It is far worse than they said." Her father shook his head as he crossed the yard.

"Someone told you?" Tessa asked.

"*Yah,* Amos Branstetter flagged me down as we came through town. Said there had been a fire at the barn, but everyone was okay." The subtle quiver in her *dat*'s voice made her stomach drop. She had caused this pain. She was the reason he was staring with disbelief at the utter destruction in front of him. Probably by morning, the last two walls would collapse into the smoldering pile of timber, reducing the barn that her grandfather had built into nothing but a memory. One that would forever be tied to her. "I misunderstood," her father continued. "This is far worse than I imagined."

"The horses are safe." Tessa grasped for something positive to report. It seemed too prideful to point out the obvious that she, too, was safe.

"*Gott is gut*," her *mem* said, staring glassy-eyed at the charred wood.

"It stinks." Joanna turned up her nose and waved a hand in front of her face. "I bet the house stinks, too."

"I opened all the windows to air it out. It's not too bad," Tessa said, eager to somehow reverse their misfortune.

"What did the fire department say? Was it a lightning strike?" her father asked. He took off his felt hat and scrubbed a hand over his messy hair. Apparently the rumor mill was already in full gear.

"The fire inspector thinks it was arson." Her pulse whooshed in her ears as she studied her father's expression. She couldn't be the reason her parents' barn had been torched, could she? She had already brought them so much pain, disappointment.

"Why would someone set our barn on fire?" Her mother spoke in a soft voice filled with disbelief. "Surely it was lightning. There was a storm." It seemed like she was trying to convince herself that the fire had been an accident, nothing nefarious.

"We'll have to get up bright and early tomorrow to clean up the remains." Her father turned toward her mother, ignoring Tessa's revelation. "The boys can help. Retrieve my tools. See what can be saved. Many hands make light work."

Surprisingly, none of her five older brothers had been by already. Maybe they were afraid to be associated with their wayward sister.

Her father's playful banter made her irrationally angry. Tessa suspected he was ready to clean up, rebuild, and move on.

Tessa wished moving on with her life could be as easy.

Joanna grabbed her Vera Bradley tote bag from the back of the van that had brought them from Syracuse. The colorful accessory was jarringly busy against her plain clothing. Tessa wondered if her little sister was biding her time until she, too, could leave the farm to buy fancy clothes and live the glamorous life. It all seemed so appealing at that age, something forbidden. But that was what *Rumspringa* was all about: to let the youths explore the outside world with the hope that experiencing it would have them running back to the Amish. In Tessa's case, it had meant running away with the first *Englisch* man who dropped down to one knee.

Her father wandered over to the van driver. Their voices carried across the field. The driver mentioned something about the Schwartz fire and God's punishment, causing her to suck in a breath. Was that the latest gossip? That God was punishing people by setting fires? Hadn't she thought the same thing? But what had the elderly Mr. and Mrs. Schwartz done?

She swallowed hard.

Her father waved to the van, then brushed past her to go inside. Tessa waited for her mother and sister to go in before following them. Once inside, Joanna pulled a newspaper out of her bag and flattened it on the kitchen table.

"Look, you made the paper," her sister announced, altogether too cheery, considering the situation.

Tessa crossed the room on shaky legs. There, spread across the spot where they'd soon share dinner, was a photo of her with the paramedics. *The photographer yesterday*. The one Sawyer had reprimanded. She pressed a hand to her chest. She looked wild-eyed in the photo. And the fact that she was wearing *Englisch* clothes wouldn't endear her to the bishop who had warned her to act contrite. She scanned the article with growing apprehension.

Tessa looked up and met her father's gaze. Then he said, "Throw that trash out, Joanna. Don't be bothering your sister with it."

A blossom of appreciation welled in her chest. Even though Joanna didn't do anything wrong, it felt good to have her *dat* in her corner for once.

"It's okay. I probably should scan the article so I know what people will be saying."

Her mother walked by and shook her head. "Pay no mind to the gossipers. You've asked for forgiveness. That's all that matters."

A new worry whispered across her brain as she planted her hands on either side of the photo that was unmistakably her. If anyone in the small town of Hunters Ridge didn't know she was back, they did now.

CHAPTER 8

For the past four months since Sawyer had been back in Hunters Ridge, he had cleared out his brother's things from their childhood home and stuffed them in the detached garage that was more like a rickety old shed. Out of sight, out of mind. Except every morning as he drank his coffee and stared out the window, he was reminded of a job left undone. A job he didn't want to do. In the meantime, Sawyer hoped the roof didn't leak and damage his brother's things, because if he came back, he'd be really irked.

If Jeb came back.

Like Tessa, Sawyer feared the worst, even though his brother's body hadn't been recovered. Part of him wondered if that was what was keeping him here. He couldn't leave until he had definitive answers about what happened.

Discovering Tessa was back in Hunters Ridge was one small piece of the puzzle, but it was still far from a complete image. Did she know more than she was letting on? Sawyer was still trying to process the fact that she was back and living among the Amish.

Why should that surprise me? She grew up Amish. But she married my brother. She's having his baby.

He took another sip of his coffee and stared out over the yard. The soft breeze through the trees sent dappled morning light into the yard. If this place was cleared out, it would really make a nice home. Maybe a vacation home for someone looking to get away from nearby Buffalo.

One of Sawyer's buddies at the fire station had encourage him to toss his brother's things into a huge bonfire, but Sawyer felt like this was the only connection with his family. His initial impetus to clean out the house had been to list the property, but then he couldn't seem to pull the trigger on that, either. Once this house was gone he'd effectively have no roots, even if the ones he had were planted in barren soil.

Sawyer set his coffee down on the counter and stepped outside. Maybe he'd go through one box a day. Small progress, but still progress. He crossed the yard, the dried leaves from last fall crunching under his footsteps. The single garage door rattled in the tracks as he pulled it open. The smell of dry cardboard and cut grass filled his nose. A soft breeze lifted his sweaty hair around his forehead, making the task a tad more tolerable.

He opened the first box labeled *main bedroom*. He smiled. There was nothing about any of the bedrooms that would make someone think it deserved that title. It had merely been his parents' bedroom once upon a time. He pulled off the lid of the first box and the strong stench of damp magazines assaulted him. He leafed through them, discovering topics including Southeast US travel, motorcycle enthusiasts, and plenty of catalogs to purchase things for adventures regarding the first two. He stuffed them back into the box and tossed it onto the gravel driveway. He'd take it into town for recycling.

"One down," he muttered to himself. By rights, he had

only promised himself he'd get rid of one box. But since it had gone well, he grabbed another. This one was marked *main cubby.*

Sawyer ran his hand over the lettering. When they were kids, he and Jeb were fascinated by all the hidden nooks and crannies in this house. Their mother's family built the cabin, but she never explained why it had so many hidden storage areas. Their father used to joke that his wife's parents were the first Amish bootleggers. As far as Sawyer knew, there was no truth to the story. It was just one more way for their drunk father to harass their beaten-down mother.

Sawyer peeled back the lid on the next box and batted aside an escaped spider. He swung at what he figured was an imaginary cobweb. He lifted what looked like a folded-up paint tarp and tossed it aside. Underneath was a zippered canvas bag. The fine hairs on the back of his neck inexplicably prickled to life. Swallowing hard, Sawyer worked his finger under the zipper and eased it back. A current of electricity raced through him. Inside he found a stack of bills. He pulled the first stack out and estimated it to be a thousand dollars. And this was just one stack.

The world went dark around the periphery of his vision as sweat beaded his forehead. He pulled out the sack of cash and set it on top of a nearby box. He peeled back another cloth layer and found a taped-up bag that made him think of the cocaine stash he'd watched the police remove from the site of a recent kitchen fire.

Sawyer blinked a few times and a *caw-caw-caw* snapped him back into the moment. He lifted his head and looked around. Apparently his only company was the crow picking at the remains of a mouse who'd gone belly-up on his driveway.

He quickly stuffed everything back into the box and set it on the driveway. He lowered the garage door and carried the box into the house where he dialed his contact at the sheriff's department, Deputy Caitlin Flagler. Feeling sicker by the minute, Sawyer sat on the front porch of his childhood home and waited for the deputy to arrive.

Deputy Caitlin Flagler parked her patrol car under the shade of a huge oak tree. Once, when they were kids, Sawyer's dad—on one of his rare good days—had fastened a huge tire swing to the largest branch. The boys had spent hours standing on the rim of the tire, one on each side, rocking and swinging, seeing who would fall off first.

Both King boys played hard, and whenever a game could be made into a competition, all the better. Their father finally cut the tire down—muttering the entire time that his sons were too stupid to live—after Jeb fell and chipped a tooth. Since they were too poor to go to the dentist, Jeb still sported a slightly jagged lower front tooth. He jokingly said it gave him character, and a good story.

The days of hanging with his little brother seemed like a lifetime ago.

The deputy climbed out of her vehicle and took in the landscape. She had done that the first time she was here in March shortly after Sawyer had come home to help search for his brother. The vegetation had been dormant and the last of the snow had yet to melt. Sawyer had missed his sister-in-law by days, according to the deputy, something that probably wouldn't have happened if he had been easier to track down. As the deputy approached, Sawyer got to his feet and waved.

The deputy planted her hands on her utility belt. "You better make sure you let me know when you're going to list this place."

He followed her gaze as she took in the gorgeous view of trees, and a pang he didn't quite want to explore made him feel hollow inside. "You and half of Hunters Ridge want this land. I think a few Amish families have their eyes on this property, too. They claim the soil here is fertile." Sawyer shrugged. "Not sure how they know. Lord knows my family never did any farming. You'd have to clear a lot of trees first."

His mother had inherited the land from her parents and had dragged her husband and two young sons to live there. His father and mother had been raised Amish. They lost their faith around the same time his father discovered alcohol, as their mother liked to say. Growing up poor in this cabin might not have been so bad if their dad wasn't a mean drunk who liked to yell at his sons for the smallest infraction—real or imagined. The happiest memory Sawyer had of this place was the morning he woke up when he was sixteen and learned that his father had bailed. Even now the memory filled him with guilt, knowing how distraught his father's betrayal had made his mother. His poor mother didn't know a good thing when it fell in her lap.

Sadly, his mother already had advanced-stage liver cancer and died a year later without even starting treatment, leaving the two King boys to run wild. Jeb, more so than Sawyer. As the older brother, Sawyer tried to be a father figure, but the boys were too close in age, and Jeb laughed at his brother's attempts at parenting him.

"Make sure you call me first," Caitlin said, turning around in a circle. "My husband would love this place. He's been fixing up a house in town. Hey, I'll be sure you get a free round of drinks at the pub every Friday for as long as you live in Hunters Ridge."

That was how Sawyer had gotten reacquainted with people in town—at the local watering hole. Something about people's jobs and official capacities were stripped away after a few beers and a game of darts. Sawyer wasn't much of a drinker; he'd nurse a beer long enough to hear what was going on in town. That was where he learned the fire department was hiring. Good thing, because it gave him a purpose and a source of income until he figured out his next step.

"No need." The smell of whiskey—his father's drink of choice—still turned his stomach. "You'll be my first call when I'm ready to sell." He probably would have been ready to list it if he had been able to make progress in his brother's disappearance. Jeb's friends weren't talking. And now that Tessa was back in town, he had extra motivation to stay. Perhaps she knew something she hadn't realized yet.

And he had a need to protect her. Had she been the target of that barn fire?

Maybe he was being paranoid. Even if he was, he lost nothing. He had a job he liked and a place to stay. If he wasn't fighting fires here, he'd be doing it someplace else. He could probably get a job anywhere. And it wasn't like he was trying to climb the corporate ladder. A skilled firefighter was a skilled firefighter. No political games, no biding his time. Work the job, go home and sleep at night. Lather, rinse, repeat.

"Hey, wait," Sawyer said. He had so much going on in his head he just realized what she had said. "Congratulations. I hadn't realized you got married."

Caitlin smiled and lifted her hand to show a simple gold band, probably the only jewelry she'd safely wear while on duty. "Decided we'd stop the tongues from wagging if we made it official. Had a small backyard ceremony back in June with our immediate families. Got the job done." She laughed; marriage obviously agreed with her. "My husband, Austin, officially left his job in Buffalo and has been updating homes. He's found his calling."

"That's great." When he first met Caitlin in March, he had heard about Special Agent Austin Grayson, who had been instrumental in taking down the preppers' compound due to their drug activity. Which brought them full circle to this moment.

"So, what's up?" The rotting porch step creaked under Caitlin's weight. She glanced down and made a face. "Yikes."

"I'll add that to my list of repairs," he said.

She shrugged. "Never ends, or at least that's what Austin says."

Sawyer held open the door. "Come on in. I want to show you something." He flipped on a light. The bare bulb glowed orange in the dimly lit space even though it was the middle of the day. He led her to the kitchen table and the cardboard box labeled *main cubby*.

Caitlin looked at the box, glanced at him, then back down at the box. "What do you have here?"

Sawyer tipped his head. "Check it out. Could be evidence."

She narrowed her gaze a fraction, then grabbed a pair of latex gloves from her back pocket. "Regarding your brother's disappearance?" she asked, sliding one glove then the other over her thin fingers. The material snapped against her wrist.

"Maybe." It felt odd to be reporting this to the sheriff's department after he had spent the years after his mother's death trying to keep his little brother out of trouble.

Caitlin lifted the lid. Sawyer's gut hurt. He felt like this was the big piece of the puzzle they had been missing. This was the reason his little brother disappeared in the middle of the night. He was into some really, really bad stuff.

The deputy repeated the actions Sawyer had before he called her. When she got to the suspected cocaine, she looked up and let out a long, low whistle. "I was afraid your brother was involved with some ruthless people." She put the lid back on the box. "I'll have to take this into evidence. They've gotten good at tracking drugs. I wouldn't be surprised if we learn this is from the same shipment Homeland Security confiscated from the compound back in February."

Sawyer didn't say anything.

"Where did you find this?" the deputy asked.

"After I moved home, I found a lot of boxes in a hidden space where my dad used to keep his liquor. I dragged most of them out to the garage."

Caitlin tipped her head toward the single-car structure, its roof in need of repair. "Any more in there?"

"I don't know. We can go check." They went back outside to the garage. He pulled up the manual door. "There's a lot of stuff in here. You might want to have a team sort through it." He chuckled even though he wasn't amused. "You'd save me the hassle of having to do it myself."

"Okay, I'll have someone come later today."

"Yeah, I want it out of here." He ran a hand roughly over his hair. "Any of the guys arrested for selling drugs last winter—the ones tied to the extremist group—any of them known to set fires?" Sawyer couldn't help but wonder if someone was retaliating against Tessa for the sins of her husband. *Surely she's not involved, too.* The idea whispered across his brain and disappeared.

No way.

Everything felt too loosely connected. He was missing something.

"Not that I heard, but I can do some checking," the deputy studied him with intelligent eyes. "You're worried the barn fire over the weekend is related since that was the Sutters' property. Is Tessa okay?"

"Yeah, a little shaken up but fine."

"Think she knew about this?" Caitlin tapped on the box with her thumb.

"No way." Heat rushed up his neck. *No way.* Had he been

too quick to defend her, just like Tessa had defended his brother?

"Because she's Amish?" Caitlin said, her tone even, her gaze scrutinizing him.

"Well, from what I understand she had to return home because she had no money. Nowhere to go. If she knew there was a stack of money stashed in her house, I think she would have made use of it." Why hadn't he thought of that earlier? The knot that was twisting in his gut eased up a bit. No way had Tessa been this stupid.

Caitlin twisted her lips, considering this. "It can't be easy for her to come back and face the community after everything she's been through."

Sawyer released a breath he hadn't realized he'd been holding. The last thing he wanted to do was cause more trouble for Tessa.

Caitlin went to leave, then paused and turned back. "One more thing. You told me when your brother first went missing that you believed he was dead."

Sawyer cleared his throat. "I had a hard time believing he'd leave his wife." He scrubbed a hand over his face.

"Now that you found this, do you still feel the same way?" The deputy had a way of asking questions that shot to the heart.

"I'll be honest with you. I hadn't talked to my brother in over two years before his death. I shouldn't presume to guess what he'd do." He let out a long huff. "But I never would have pegged him to be dealing drugs."

"No one suspects their loved ones." Caitlin tucked the box under one arm. "You realize I'm going to need to talk to Tessa Sutter now, right? She also lived in this house." The deputy had been paying close attention to Tessa, even knowing that she had gone back to her maiden name.

"I was worried about that," Sawyer said. "Would you let

me pick her up and bring her into the station? If you show up on her family's farm, she'll suffer the consequences of my brother's actions."

"You're pretty confident she has nothing to do with this."

"I'd bet my life on it."

CHAPTER 9

Later that day Sawyer drove to the farm where Tessa had grown up and couldn't help but feel like he was intruding. Probably because he was. Outsiders were rarely welcomed, especially when he was the brother of the man who had taken Tessa away from her Amish faith.

Across the yard, a dozen or so Amish men picked up charred wood from the heap and tossed it to a worn patch of earth. From there, another man stacked it onto the back of a wagon. Fortunately for Sawyer, he and his team had already collected evidence. Definitely an accelerant and broken glass. Someone had intentionally set this fire. Now it was up to the sheriff's department to figure out who. And he had been around the Amish long enough to know this would be no easy task. They liked to remain separate and would be reluctant to talk to the sheriff's department.

Seemed quiet Hunters Ridge had a rash of crimes on their hands.

Even though it would be easier to approach Tessa when he didn't have the eyes of several Amish men on him, this couldn't wait. He had to find out what was going on to determine if Tessa was being targeted. If she stayed here, she'd be in danger.

Sawyer gave a quick wave to the men. It seemed like the logical thing to do since they were staring. Only one waved back. The rest dipped their heads as if gawking was something to be ashamed about. Sawyer didn't care if they wanted to stare. He was on a mission. He headed directly toward the house and slowed when he heard someone opening the door. Tessa appeared with a glass pitcher of lemonade.

Her mouth formed a perfect O upon seeing him. Her eyes immediately narrowed, then her gaze drifted to the men across the field. He hated that his showing up here was causing her stress. Nothing about their interactions ever seemed to be simple.

"I'm sorry to bother you," Sawyer said, and he genuinely was. He had no intention of hurting her.

She shifted her stance and the wind blew the fabric of her plain dress against her belly, revealing her small baby bump. He quickly lifted his gaze and smiled tightly, feeling voyeuristic. That had never been his intent. "Can we talk?"

Tessa hoisted the lemonade. "I have to take this to the workers." There was a sad look in her eyes and a stack of paper cups tucked under her arm.

Sawyer held out his hands. "Let me."

"That's not a good idea."

Her mother appeared in the doorway behind Tessa, her guarded expression tough to read. "Is something wrong?"

Tessa shook her head tightly. Sawyer took that as his cue to speak up. "We'd like to ask your daughter a few more questions about the fire." He made it sound more official than it really was.

"More questions? I think she's answered them all." Worry lines creased the corners of her mother's eyes, reminding him of the constant pressure on his own mother when she was left to raise two boys, knowing that she was dying.

"Just a few more." Sawyer hated lying, but he couldn't shrug his shoulders and leave Tessa here unprotected. Maybe he was being paranoid, but he couldn't take that chance. Jeb's disappearance and this fire might be related, especially because she had been in the barn at the time it was set. He wasn't about to wait for Tessa to fall victim again so he could make a definitive connection.

"Let me take this." Mrs. Sutter took the pitcher from her daughter and sighed heavily, obviously accustomed to assuming the responsibilities of others. She tucked the cups under her arm, like Tessa had done. "The men are thirsty while you stand here gabbing." For the briefest of moments, Sawyer thought he saw a spark of amusement in her eyes, but he was probably mistaken. The King boys had brought nothing but trouble to the Sutters.

"Mem..."

The single word trailed off, as if delivering the lemonade had been Tessa's only excuse to get away from him.

They watched her mother walk away, then Tessa crossed her arms over her chest. "I've told you everything. I heard a crash. There was a thunderstorm. Then the fire." She made a show of being bored with the story, then lifted her gaze to his. Something behind her eyes softened. She drew in a deep breath and exhaled. "I'm sorry. I'm tired. And every time an outsider comes here because of me, I get grief from my parents." She angled her chin toward where the barn once stood. Most of the men were now taking a lemonade break and staring in their direction. "Now the rumor mill will crank up again about me." She gave him a sad smile. "I don't like being the subject of gossip."

Sawyer hated that he had to be the one to bring her the news he had come to share. "We have to talk." She dipped her head and he studied the top of her bonnet and waited for her to meet his gaze. "It's about Jeb," he added.

She shook her head, as if trying to escape the nightmare she was living in. "I don't know what else I can tell you that I haven't told every person who has been out looking for him since he disappeared."

"Please. It's important." He glanced up at the house, unsure of who else was around.

Worry flashed in her eyes. "You're scaring me."

"That's not my intention, but I discovered something at the cabin today." He wanted to reach out, touch her arm, but he wouldn't do that to her, not in front of an audience. Just being here was bad enough.

"What did you find?" Her chest started to heave with anxiety.

"Would you come with me to the sheriff's department?" he asked. Her face fired pink and he tried to determine if she had any inkling what he was talking about. If perhaps she was involved with the drugs, too.

"The sheriff's department? Why?" Tessa's voice shook.

"Deputy Caitlin Flagler needs a statement from you." Maybe the deputy was going by a different last name now that she was married, but she hadn't mentioned it.

"A statement?" Confusion and frustration laced her tone. "Okay, fine," she said, resigned. "Let's go. If the townspeople are going to talk about me, we might as well make it good."

CHAPTER 10

Tessa followed Deputy Caitlin Flagler into a conference room, keenly aware of Sawyer right behind her, the warmth of his firm hand hovering over the small of her back. Every nerve ending was on fire. Sawyer had insisted they wait until they were at the station before he revealed what he had found, and her anxiety had only grown, making her feel queasy.

Jeb, what did you do? Once again, the niggling feeling that she had married a stranger twisted her up inside. She was on the verge of tears but she refused to let them fall. Tessa had felt the eyes of her father's friends on her as she walked to Sawyer's truck. Now she sensed the employees in the sheriff's department staring at her. She didn't imagine it was often they had a woman in a bonnet strolling through their offices, despite working in a heavily Amish town.

She was tired of being gawked at.

Feeling exhausted and out of place had become a theme in her life.

"Have a seat," the deputy said. The woman's hair was a

pretty shade of red that was swept up in a low bun. Tessa wondered if they could have been friends in another life.

"Thank you," Tessa said quietly. She pulled the chair up to the table and tried not to fidget with her hands clasped in her lap. "I don't know why I'm here," she said as Sawyer pulled out a chair and sat next to her. The deputy remained standing. "I've told you everything about the fire and about Jeb's disappearance. I don't know anything else."

"There's been a new development," the deputy said, her lips flattening into a straight line. Her tone suggested she was sympathetic to Tessa's plight.

"Do you have news about my husband?" Tessa couldn't keep her voice from shaking. Was that why Sawyer was being evasive? He hadn't the heart to tell her they had found Jeb's body?

Sawyer placed his hand on her arm. "No, it's not what you think. Take a deep breath. It'll be okay."

Tessa drew in a shaky breath. "Please stop dragging this out. Tell me why I'm here."

The deputy bent over and picked up a box from the floor and set it on the conference room table in front of her. A musty smell made her scrunch her nose. "Does this look familiar?" the deputy asked.

Tessa could feel the weight of the deputy's stare. "No, should it?" She angled her head to make out the writing. "What's a cubby?"

The deputy and Sawyer shared a look and he was the first to speak up. "It's a small hidden storage nook."

"You found it at the cabin." It was more a statement than a question.

"Yes. I was cleaning out the cabin and stumbled across this."

"I had no idea there was a storage area in there. Where exactly was it?" She leaned back and palmed the arms of her chair, feeling her hands grow sweaty. Whatever was in that box had landed her here.

Whatever is in the box was put in there by my husband.

"Inside the closet in the main bedroom," Sawyer explained.

Caitlin put on gloves and opened the box. "Tell me if anything looks familiar."

Tessa stared wide-eyed as the deputy unpacked the box. She felt like she was floating above her body. The deputy removed one stack of bills after another. Tessa swallowed hard. "That was in our house?" Her lower lip trembled. "Whose money is that?"

"That's what we're trying to figure out," the deputy said. "Was your husband into anything illegal?"

"No," Tessa said sharply. "Absolutely not." Her mind flashed back to making the same argument to Sawyer not long ago. But how well did she really know her husband? Did he deserve her unconditional support?

Does it even matter, if he is dead?

The thought made tears prick the back of her eyes.

The deputy pulled out a packet of something. Instinctively Tessa lifted her hand, but the deputy shifted, keeping it out of reach. "Please don't touch. It's evidence."

"What is it?" Tessa asked, hating the squeak in her voice.

"A sample has been sent out for testing, but we believe it's cocaine, perhaps from the same supply they confiscated from the preppers compound this past winter."

Tessa grew dizzy and a bead of sweat rolled down between her shoulder blades.

"Is there any way Jeb got involved with this group?" Sawyer asked, his voice close to her ear. His familiar scent reached her nose, reminding her of a long-ago time—shortly after she had met the King brothers—when she had too much to drink at some party. She had stepped outside to get fresh air. Jeb stayed inside with his friends pounding back one beer after another. It was Sawyer who came to check on her. See if she was okay. Offered her a ride home. Tessa had told him she'd be fine with Jeb, that he'd take care of her.

That wasn't the only time she had wondered if she was with the wrong brother. She closed her eyes briefly and pushed the thought aside.

"He would never do that." She hated that she sounded like she was pleading for them to believe her.

"I found it in a place only he knew about," Sawyer said.

Tessa swiveled around to glare at him. "But *you* knew about it." She lashed out at him, feeling defensive.

Sawyer stared at her with hurt in his eyes. Her face grew warm. He hadn't deserved that.

"Did you have any knowledge of this, Tessa?" the deputy asked, putting the contents back into the box and closing the lid.

"Do you think if I knew I had that kind of money that I would have moved back home to my Amish parents?" She sniffed, feeling indignant, hurt, confused. "I had no idea it was in there." She looked to Sawyer. "Do you think he could have done this?" His brother had known Jeb for twenty-some years. She had only known him for a couple. And her husband had seemed edgy in the days and weeks leading up to his disappearance.

"I don't know," he said. The honesty in his eyes was plainly clear. The truth of the matter was, she didn't know either. "I do know he cared for you, and it wouldn't be unlike my brother to do whatever it took to provide for you."

"I told him a million times that I had everything I needed." Tessa pointed at the box. "If he was involved with that, it wasn't because I put pressure on him."

"No one is saying that," Deputy Flagler said. "We just

needed to ask you a few questions. See what you knew. What you remembered."

"I knew nothing about that. You have to believe me." Her heart thrummed in her ears and the walls of the conference room felt like they were closing in on her. Was she going to be in trouble for this?

Sawyer covered her hand and squeezed. The deputy smiled. "There's no reason to believe you were involved."

Tessa sensed an "unless new information is uncovered" was left unsaid, but she took the deputy at her word. Tessa needed to hold on to whatever hope she could.

"Sadly, I didn't know Jeb as well as I thought I did." She looked up with a spark of hope. "Is there any chance someone planted it there after he disappeared?"

"Maybe, but not likely. Sawyer said he moved that box out of its small hiding place to the detached garage months ago."

"After Jeb disappeared, I felt like someone had been through our things when I wasn't home. I reported the incident, but there was no evidence of a break-in. It seemed like a few things had been moved and put back, but not exactly in the right spot." She dragged a hand over her head and pulled off her bonnet. She folded the fabric in her hands. "I thought I was losing my mind. I had to leave after that. I didn't want to be alone there anymore."

"We'll have to go back through all the people Jeb associated with," the deputy said, and Tessa sagged into the chair. "No, don't worry, we already have a list. We'll push them a little harder for information in light of this discovery."

"Okay..." Tessa set her bonnet down on the table.

"If your husband was dealing drugs, he would have been involved with some very bad people," the deputy said, meeting her gaze directly. "I don't mean to alarm you, but it might explain his disappearance. And perhaps one of these people is looking to retaliate against you."

"Why?" Tessa's pulse whooshed in her ears. "I had no idea."

Sawyer covered her hand with his. "They might believe otherwise."

"If your goal wasn't to alarm me, you've failed." Tessa laughed, a mirthless sound. She looked at the deputy, then Sawyer. "You think I'm in serious danger, don't you? No more question about it."

"I'm afraid so," Sawyer said.

Tessa pulled her hand away from his and rubbed her forehead. "What am I supposed to do?" She looked at the deputy because she feared if she met Sawyer's sympathetic gaze, she might break down in tears.

"We can put you someplace safe," the deputy suggested. "I'd have to run it up the department first, but yeah, we can figure something out."

"Or you could come home with me," Sawyer suggested.

Tessa shot him a gaze. "With you? To the cabin? Wouldn't that be the most obvious place they'd look for me?"

"I can keep you safe there."

Sawyer locked eyes with her, and in that moment she believed him. But how was she supposed to explain her living arrangements to her parents when she had already come home on bended knee asking for forgiveness for her transgressions?

Sawyer must have sensed the turmoil swirling around within her. "You can worry about your family and what the bishop thinks later. The most important thing is to keep you..." He hesitated for a brief moment. "And my niece or nephew safe."

Subconsciously she put her hand on her growing belly and nodded. "Okay, but can I get a few things from home first?"

CHAPTER 11

Sawyer sensed the shift in mood as soon as they arrived at Tessa's family's farm after going to the sheriff's department. Trying to strike an optimistic tone, he said, "Get what you need. I'll wait right here."

Tessa bit her lower lip and stared out the window at the buzz of activity around the barn raising. She reached for the door handle but didn't open it. "Maybe this is a bad idea." She didn't look at him. Perhaps she couldn't.

"Tessa," he tried to reason, "we don't know who Jeb was involved with. We don't know who set the fire. You're not safe here." So much for being optimistic.

She shifted in her seat. "The last thing I want to do is bring danger to my family." She sniffed. "I already feel horrible about that fire. But who is going to try anything when half the town is here?" Her words poured out in a rush, as if she had just figured it all out. Rationalized it.

"They're not here 24-7," Sawyer said. "Please, come with me where I can keep an eye on you."

Tessa stared straight ahead and something seemed to register. Her face flushed a bright red and her jaw grew slack.

"The bishop is here." She pulled on the door latch. "I have to go."

"Tessa," Sawyer called.

She paused, holding the door open. "The last thing I want to do is hurt my family, but if I go with you, I'll never be welcomed home again. I made a promise to the bishop. I asked for forgiveness for breaking the rules." Her lower lip began to quiver. She glanced over at the approaching bishop, her father at his side. Sawyer couldn't imagine the pressure she was under.

Sawyer reached for his door handle. "I can—"

The passenger side door slammed shut before he finished his sentence. He had to explain. Let them know Tessa's life was in danger.

Tessa rushed ahead and called over her shoulder. "Thanks for driving me home. I'm all set now." Panic rolled off her in waves and Sawyer hated how she had to live like this, always trying to please someone else. But then again, he had to respect the Amish; they did look out for their own. Someone like Sawyer would have loved more support after his mother died.

Shaking off his meandering thoughts, he kept following her even though he suspected he was pushing her toward the lion's den.

Surely they'll understand.

"What's going on, Tessa?" her father barked.

Tessa glanced over and something flitted in the depths of her eyes when she realized Sawyer was right behind her. This is what betrayal must feel like. He had to risk it. He'd apologize profusely later.

"Um," Tessa said, dipping her head, "I had to give another statement to the sheriff's department about the fire. They're trying to figure out who started it."

The bishop ran his hand down his long, wiry beard.

"Have you forgotten the agreement we made?" He lifted his cane a fraction for emphasis, and Sawyer suspected he might have waved it at her if he hadn't needed it for stability.

Her father lowered his gaze. Sawyer wished he'd defend his daughter.

"*Neh,* Bishop Leroy. I haven't. But don't you want to catch the person who did this?" She held up her palm to the structure that was quickly going up in place of the old barn.

The bishop rattled his cane. "*Gott* will be the judge. You need to leave worldly things for the outsiders." The elderly bishop tipped his head at Sawyer. "It would be best if you stop coming around. We can look out for our own."

"Sir—" Sawyer started.

"I'll be fine here," Tessa said, turning to Sawyer. "You'll have to go. I have made a promise that I need to honor."

Sawyer wondered if her father could see the pain in her eyes. Or had his upbringing allowed him to ignore it because in the end, his daughter had to remain faithful to the *Ordnung* or risk eternal damnation? Sawyer had heard enough about the teachings of the Amish through his parents, former Amish who struggled to fully transition to the outside world. So who was he to force Tessa?

"Are you sure?" He looked around. The men who had been busy hammering had paused to watch the interaction between Tessa and the bishop. He mentally cursed himself. If only he had come back after the men had stopped working for the night, spared her from a public shaming.

"I know I'm safe here. I'll be with my family," Tessa said, barely above a whisper.

Reluctantly, Sawyer took a step backward. He didn't have a choice. He wanted to have a word with her in private, but he knew that wouldn't happen. "Please don't go anywhere alone." He locked gazes with her and waited for a nod of understanding. He could read the apology in her eyes, but out of respect for her wishes he turned on his heel and strode back to his truck.

Once inside, he watched her mother approach, hold out her hand, and direct her daughter into the house. Tessa glanced over her shoulder at him for the briefest of moments. How was he ever going to reach her?

He tapped the steering wheel with his fist. How had he lost control of this situation? The men had gone back to work, yet he had an uneasy feeling that someone was watching him. His gaze swept over the workers, one by one, to determine if someone was paying him particular attention. But it was impossible to tell, their faces obscured by the shadows of their broad-brimmed hats.

Suddenly the four walls of Tessa's childhood home felt suffocating. The open windows allowed minimal air flow on the hot summer day. She wanted to run upstairs to the privacy of her bedroom and figure out how her day had gone so horribly wrong, but the uninsulated second story would be over-the-top oppressive. Instead, she got a glass of water, and collapsed into a kitchen chair and tried not to make eye contact with her mother.

Tessa was done talking for the day.

Her mother, perhaps realizing her daughter was struggling, offered to make her something to eat. Tessa refused. The last thing she wanted to do in this heat was eat.

"Maybe a glass of lemonade on the porch will help," her mother said. When Tessa didn't answer, her mother added, "There's a little breeze."

The idea of sitting on the porch like she was on display wasn't any more appealing than most of her other limited options. How had she ended up in this situation? One false step after another. Was this what her life had become? It was hard to soothe her growing frustration.

"I'll join you," her mother coaxed. "I have a minute before I need to start prepping the next meal." Her mother's life seemed to be a series of short breaks between various chores.

Is this the life I'm prepared to live?

"I can help you," Tessa said automatically. She had grown up in this environment, and even though she had been living as an outsider for the past few years, the rules and way of life weren't something she could easily turn off. Hadn't she been a good wife to Jeb—making him dinner, keeping his house clean, and not questioning his authority? How was her mother's life any different? Maybe it was time she stopped fighting her preordained path in life.

She blinked slowly, trying to clear her mind. Her entire body ached. Her limbs and heart were heavy. Maybe it was the heat. Maybe it was her pregnancy. Or maybe it was the no-win situation she found herself in. Maybe it was a combination of everything.

Tessa had agreed to stay here in her parents' house after the bishop strong-armed her when she returned with Sawyer. Was she doing the right thing in not protesting? Per the rules of the *Ordnung*, she was. Since she had sought forgiveness, she must now walk the walk even though she feared with every inch of her being that she was putting her family in danger.

But from whom?

"Come on." Her mother tipped her head toward the door, holding two glasses of lemonade, condensation dripping from their sides. Tessa rushed ahead of her and opened the door.

The two women sat down. The overhang provided blessed shade from the relentless afternoon sun. And her mother was right. There was a soft breeze.

"*Denki*," Tessa said, accepting the drink. The ice clacked when she lifted the glass to her lips. The lemonade was tart and refreshing and reminded her of her childhood. In that moment, an overwhelming sense of homesickness washed over her. She had to clear the emotion from her throat before she spoke. "I don't mean to cause so much trouble."

"You'll find your way." The empathy in her mother's tone almost made Tessa cry, especially because Tessa would break her mother's heart if she left again.

She drew in a deep breath and let it out. She wished she had as much confidence as her mother. No, what she needed was faith, something her mother seemed to have in abundance.

"The men are making short work of the barn," her mother said, giving her daughter a reprieve from the emotions that were hovering right below the surface. Across the yard, Joanna was collecting the empty glasses in a basket, throwing the occasional glance in their direction.

"They are," Tessa said, staring blindly in the direction of the construction. Her mother had made many mentions of counting her blessings. The barn had burned down, but now *Gott* had provided them with a new one. Her mother was the ultimate positive thinker. She had complete faith in God's providence.

A tall, thin man broke away from a group of construction workers at the corner of the barn where they had been taking their lemonade break. Tessa's heart jolted when she realized he was walking in their direction. He had covered half the space between the new barn and the house when she recognized Deacon Bontrager. A surge of adrenaline coursed through her, clouding her brain. *Stay or go. Fight or flight.* She had dealt with his kind all too often, especially after she married Jeb. The "holier-than-thous" as Jeb called them, liked to give witness to her in the grocery store or at the diner.

Repent or you'll burn in hell. That from the older crowd.

Sinner! Sinner! was usually the chant from those who remembered she had done something wrong but couldn't know exactly what.

Go down on bended knee.

She had avoided downtown, but now one of the biggest mouths had come to her. Just her luck. The heat pressed in on all sides and she feared she was going to pass out.

Sensing her apprehension, her mother said in a familiar, soothing voice, the one she used when one of her children had fallen and hurt themselves, "It's okay. The deacon has been coming around a bit. I think he wants to get to know us better. His son Camp has been taking Joanna home from Sunday singings." Her mother was definitely pleased by this development. And so was Joanna.

Tessa didn't have time to let her thoughts drift to familiar what-ifs.

What if I *had found a nice Amish man and settled down?*

What if I *had never met Jeb?*

What if—

"Hello, Mrs. Sutter. The lemonade is very refreshing." Deacon Bontrager took off his Amish hat and ran the back of his hand over his sweaty forehead.

"*Denki*," her mother replied, her chest swelling with pride before she seemed to catch herself and settle back in the chair. She held out her hand. "Our daughter is back staying with us." A surge of affection warmed Tessa's heart. It meant a lot to her that her mother was acknowledging her and not telling her to hide for fear of what people will say.

However Tessa couldn't miss the slight purse to the deacon's lips before he formed a smile that didn't reach his eyes. "I haven't had the pleasure of welcoming you home." His gaze dropped to her belly, then over his shoulder to the barn.

"Hello, Mr. Bontrager. Your son Camp was by the other day. And I believe your older sons are close to my age."

"*Yah,* and you're back for *gut?*" His gave her a withering look. It must have been something every leader in the church thought they needed to perfect.

"You know what they say, 'Humans plan and *Gott* laughs.'" She smiled smugly and instantly regretted it. Petulance wasn't a good look on anyone.

"We are thankful to have Tessa home," her mother said, forever the polite woman that she had been raised to be.

"A blessing for sure," he said, an iciness to his tone that set Tessa's teeth on edge.

"Can I get you more lemonade?" her mother asked, sliding to the edge of her chair.

"*Neh, neh,* I wanted to say hello." He smiled tightly, then turned around and walked back to the barn.

"What was that all about?" Tessa asked, wondering if the interaction was being colored by her awful day.

"No need to be rude," her mother said. "I think that's his way of getting a sense of our family since his son has been courting your sister. We have our own way of doing things."

The Amish did. They didn't openly discuss engagements, until they happened. Tessa didn't understand a lot of what her family and neighbors did. Maybe she'd never understand.

Taking a long drink of her lemonade, she let her gaze drift over to where Mr. Bontrager lingered among the workers. Now that she had seen him up close, his tall, thin frame was easy to spot. Despite the distance and the shadow of his broad-brimmed hat, she was certain he was staring at her. An icy chill raced up her spine despite the line of sweat along her hairline.

CHAPTER 12

Tessa's mother stood. "I need to prepare dinner."

Tessa palmed the arms of the rocker. "I'll help you."

"*Neh,* sit. Relax. I don't have much to do."

Alone outside, Tessa leaned her head back and closed her eyes and started to doze. She had no idea how she was going to stay awake for the last few months of her pregnancy. She was so tired.

Heavy footsteps on the porch startled Tessa. It took her a heartbeat to orient herself. Thankfully, it was only her little sister. Joanna plunked the basket of empty glasses on the porch and leaned back on the railing. "What did he say?" she asked excitedly.

Tessa loved a good nap, but hated that fuzzy, groggy feeling from being jolted awake. She plucked at the fabric of her dress and narrowed her gaze. "Who said what?"

Joanna huffed in frustration. "Camp's *dat*? Who else? Did he say anything about me?"

The hope and eagerness in her little sister's eyes did something funny to Tessa's insides. Something about the

Bontrager family rubbed her the wrong way, and she couldn't understand her sister's interest in them. Or maybe she could. Tessa had been young once, and any attention, especially from boys, was exciting. Differentiating between good-exciting and bad-exciting would only come with maturity.

Something Tessa learned too late.

"Oh, he just wanted to say thank you for the lemonade, I guess." Tessa struggled to remember the exact exchange that had left her feeling a bit unsettled. But maybe that hadn't been Mr. Bontrager's fault. Feeling uneasy had been a state of being for Tessa lately.

"Did you tell him I squeezed the lemons? Added just the right amount of sugar like Mem taught us?" Joanna asked, practically bouncing on the balls of her black boots.

"I'm sorry. I didn't. I didn't honestly have much to say. Mem did say she thought he wanted to say hello because he knows Camp has been courting you."

Joanna drew her hands to her chest and did a mini clap with the pads of her fingers, practically squealing. "Did Mem really say that?"

Tessa remembered being smitten with a local boy when she was about Joanna's age, but the feeling had quickly faded when she realized that even though he had handsome eyes and thick hair and, well, was easy on the eyes, they had little in common. What if she had rushed into marriage and realized that too late?

It's not like you took the long road before marrying Jeb.

"Yah." Tessa smiled. "She did. I almost couldn't believe it myself." It felt great to share some girl talk with her sister. She had missed her.

"Mem never wants to talk about boys." Joanna pressed her palm to her forehead and glanced around, as if trying to digest this bit of information. Tessa could practically hear her younger sister's thoughts: *They were talking about me! Me!*

A smile pulled at the corners of Tessa's lips. "That's just her way. Mem and Dat might not say it, but they want what's best for their children." They had gone above and beyond in allowing Tessa to return home after she had broken half the rules laid out in the *Ordnung*. They deserved credit for that.

"What do you think of Camp?" Joanna slid into the rocker next to hers and leaned heavily on the arm. Her excitement rolled off her in waves.

"I can't say I really know him." Tessa was careful to keep her expression neutral. She didn't want to pop her sister's bubble by telling her she didn't care for his brothers. But if she didn't tell her little sister, who would? She straightened the fabric of her dress, buying time to select her words carefully. If she came off too critical, her sister would lash out, call her mean. Perhaps tell her she didn't know anything, and who could blame her. It wasn't like Tessa had been a pillar of the community. How much weight could her opinion hold anyway?

Before she had a chance to give her sister some backstory on the self-righteous Bontrager family, a loud muffler drew their attention to the road. A beat-up car turned into their driveway. It didn't strike her as a hired car for one of the Amish workers. Tessa squinted and her heart dropped when the driver climbed out.

The visitor was for her.

Heather Kelly, a friend—no, an acquaintance—from her former life strolled toward the house while taking long glances at the barn going up. Tessa wasn't sure if the woman saw her sitting on the porch or was just heading toward the house.

"Do you know her?" Joanna asked.

"Mmmhmmm...Heather...." Even though Tessa had no

idea what brought this woman here, she wanted her to turn around and leave. She didn't want to know anything more about the life she had left or the one Jeb had potentially gotten mixed up with.

"Heather's giving the workers an eyeful," her little sister said under her breath.

Joanna wasn't wrong. The jean short-shorts and the white tank top that stopped shy of covering her belly button were far from conservative in the *Englisch* world, but among the Amish, the outfit was downright scandalous. "Don't judge, lest you be judged," she whispered, sympathetic to what it was like to be the subject of gossip.

"Oh, I'm not judging. I'm just looking." Joanna laughed. They watched the woman pick her steps carefully across the rutted yard as if the grooves were much deeper than they were.

"I have no idea why she's here." Tessa pushed up from the rocker and strolled toward the top of the steps.

Heather looked up and the deep lines in her forehead smoothed when she saw Tessa. The visitor waved heartily. "There you are! I was afraid maybe I had the wrong place." Heather stopped on the bottom step, took one flip-flop off, wiped her foot with the palm of her hand, then slid it back on. She repeated the action for the other foot. It seemed pointless considering she'd have to follow the same path when she returned to her car.

"You found me," Tessa said, the ever-present knot in her gut growing tighter. Now that her "old friend" stood inches away, Tessa noticed the bottom edge of the white pockets peeking out from under her very short jean shorts. Tessa felt her face flush.

The *Englischer* ascended the steps and surprised Tessa by pulling her into a tight embrace, then straightened her arms to study her. "Look at you, honey. I hardly recognized you..."

She touched one of the dangling bonnet strings and tilted her head and frowned. "Back to your Amish roots."

Tessa reflexively stepped backward, feeling the scrutiny of the woman. "After Jeb...well, I didn't have much choice."

"I was so worried about you," Heather continued.

"I'm fine." Tessa didn't know what to say, especially with half the Amish community of Hunters Ridge watching them. It didn't help that her sister was only a few feet away and all ears.

Heather fanned herself. A bead of sweat formed on her upper lip. "It's like a sauna out here, and you with that long dress." She plucked at the cape and Tessa was getting annoyed at how handsy this woman was. Tessa clasped her hands over her midsection, hoping to hide her pregnancy. "You must be roasting."

Tessa took another step back, reclaiming her personal space. "It's what you're used to I suppose." Feeling scatter-brained at this woman's sudden appearance, she held out her palm. "This is my sister Joanna."

"Ah..." Heather smiled. "Mini Tessa." She pulled her sister into a hug.

Joanna raised her eyebrows and shot her sister a look over Heather's shoulder. Apparently unsure of what to do with her arms, Joanna decided to let them dangle awkwardly by her sides. The Amish were not an overly demonstrative group.

"You guys are practically twins," Heather said.

Heather released Joanna who stumbled backward and laughed, seemingly entertained by the exchange.

"What brings you here?" Tessa asked, feeling the eyes of the workers on her again. However, Joanna was probably right. This time they were watching the *Englischer* who was dressed far more sensibly for the weather than either of the women in their long dresses.

"I'm so glad you're okay. I saw your photograph in the paper with that horrible barn fire." Heather waved her hand in the general direction of the barn. "Look at those men go. I've never seen a barn raising in person." She planted her hands on her fists and stared out over the yard.

"Yes, everything's fine." Tessa's first reaction was to be annoyed at the invasion of privacy that photo had created, but deep down a flicker of something else—hope, maybe—grew that perhaps this woman could provide answers. This interaction would have never occurred if Heather didn't know where to find her.

"I had no idea you were back in Hunters Ridge," Heather said, interrupting Tessa's thoughts. "You left so quickly after poor Jeb went missing. I thought you disappeared too."

A trickle of sweat rolled down Tessa's back. She didn't know Heather well enough to go into the details of the worst night of her life, then to the subsequent discovery she was pregnant, to moving away and then back again. She settled on a simple, "Well, I'm back."

"I'm so glad." There was an over-the-top quality to her tone that rubbed Tessa the wrong way. It wasn't like they were going to become besties now.

"Thank you," Tessa replied all the same. She turned to Joanna and said, "Would you mind getting us some of your famous lemonade?"

"Sure," Joanna said flatly, disappointed her sister was shooing her away.

"Oh, wait!" Heather reached into her tote bag and pulled out a cellophane-wrapped item. "I brought you guys some homemade pumpkin bread. I heard the Amish loved their baked goods."

Tessa thanked her and handed the package to her sister. "That was nice of you." She felt overly self-conscious. Why was this woman here? It was like bringing her recent past right into the heart of her present—and her future.

Heather watched Joanna disappear inside. "Oh good, I need to talk to you in private and I don't have much time." It was then that Tessa realized she wasn't the only one who was nervous.

"Oh." Did she have news of her husband? The two women had been friendly, but not overly. Tessa had always suspected Heather held something against her because she was former Amish. Or maybe Tessa was projecting.

"Where did you go after Jeb left? Eddie and I stopped by the cabin after the accident, and you were gone."

"I couldn't stay in that cabin alone."

"Are you going to go back?"

"To the cabin?" She shook her head. "His brother lives there now."

Heather gave a subtle nod, as if she had settled something. "You've gone back to being Amish? For good?"

In that moment, she wanted to share her news with someone who knew her with Jeb. Knew how much they loved each other. Knew her as Jeb's wife. "I..." She glanced toward the door and window to make sure no one was eavesdropping. "I'm pregnant."

Heather's hands flew to her mouth. "OMG!"

Tessa bristled at her casual exclamation. "Yeah, and I don't exactly have the skills to get a job to support us."

"You'll raise the baby Amish? Wow! I'm happy for you." Heather was probably the first person who sounded genuinely happy.

Tessa tilted her head and smiled. She couldn't voice her plans to give the baby to her brother because she wasn't convinced she'd be able to go through with it. She rubbed her growing baby bump. Either way, time was running out.

"Did you, um, have a chance to move your things from

the cabin?" the woman asked. It seemed like a strange question.

"Just my personal things. I kept thinking Jeb would come back." Tessa's pulse thrummed in her ears at her admission.

"You left everything behind?" There was a hint of disbelief in Heather's tone.

Tessa shrugged. "I don't need much." She studied the woman. "Is that why you came here? To ask about my living situation?"

Heather waved her hand, but the attempt at being casual seemed forced. "I was worried about you. That's all."

Tessa's mind raced. How would she frame this? "Do you know where Jeb was going the night he disappeared?"

Something flashed in the depths of Heather's eyes that Tessa couldn't quite decipher. "I don't know. Eddie never understood why Jeb claimed that he had called him up for a late-night delivery."

"Someone texted him that night." Her stomach knotted whenever she relived the details of her last exchange with her husband. She should have insisted he stay home even though she knew in her heart that she didn't have that kind of power over him.

"I don't think it was Eddie." Heather's voice squeaked and she averted her gaze.

"Please don't take this the wrong way, but was Eddie involved in anything illegal?" The stack of money and drugs Sawyer uncovered came to mind.

Heather's eyes jumped to hers and flashed dark. "No, of course not." Heather's reaction was similar to Tessa's when Sawyer mentioned the drugs to her. "Don't even suggest something like that. Eddie works hard to grow his business." She scoffed. "He'd never do that."

Feeling her face grow hot again, Tessa held up her hands

and backtracked. "I'm sorry. I'm desperate to know what happened to Jeb."

Why does Heather want to know if I removed things from the cabin?

Tessa dismissed the unsettling thought. "Jeb seemed harried the night he disappeared." She was mostly thinking aloud. "And then the accident on the ice."

Heather made a tsking noise. "I can't imagine how hard all this must be for you..."

"I'm doing okay." Silence stretched between them for a beat. "Thank you for stopping by to check on me," Tessa said out of politeness, but something seemed off.

"Can I visit again?" Tessa couldn't tell if Heather's enthusiasm was an act.

No, that wouldn't be appropriate. "Sure, I'd like that."

Maybe eventually Tessa would get to the bottom of what Jeb was up to the night he disappeared. And deep in her gut, she suspected Eddie and his girlfriend, Heather, knew more than they were letting on.

CHAPTER 13

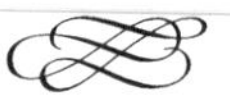

"I wonder why they haven't rebuilt," Sawyer said to the deputy as they pulled onto the Schwartzes' property. A large patch of scorched earth in the outline of a barn sat untouched near the tree line at the back of their property.

"Me too," Caitlin said. "Did you have a chance to go through the files on this one?" She reached for the door handle of his personal vehicle. Both of them were off duty, in the hopes that the Amish family would be more receptive to talking to them about the fire that had destroyed their barn a couple months ago.

"Yeah, not a lot of info," Sawyer said, climbing out of the truck and meeting Caitlin around front. "I helped fight the fire. It was a raging inferno. My money would have been on arson, but the captain said it's not uncommon with these old barns. The wood is dry and we've been in a drought."

"Let me guess, the investigation stopped dead in the water when the Amish homeowners refused to cooperate," the deputy said, having had her own experience with the Amish's need to stay separate, and that included avoiding law enforcement.

"Exactly. The family—an older couple, if I remember correctly, were more than grateful that we saved their surrounding buildings and property, but then they wanted us gone."

"Seems they wanted the charred wood gone, too," Caitlin said as they approached the black earth. She dragged the toe of her sneaker through a patch, leaving a line. "Not much by way of evidence."

Sawyer tented his hand over his eyes and glanced toward the house. "Let's see what they have to say today."

"You are far more optimistic than me." Caitlin laughed and ran her hand down her long ponytail. "But that's why we came, right? New day. New approach." Sawyer had come to respect the deputy highly. She was smart, thorough, yet easy-going. A rare combination in law enforcement, in his experience. She'd go far.

The Schwartzes had refused to allow anyone to inspect the ruins after the fire and the fire department had accepted the act-of-nature excuse, considering there had been a storm that night, too. Perhaps a calculated risk by a clever arsonist.

Or maybe Sawyer had grown too jaded fighting fires out west where the lack of forethought—or plain stupidity—on the part of mankind had destroyed acre upon acre of forest.

The dry grass crunched under Sawyer's feet as he crossed the property to the main house. He was struck by how quiet it was. No animals or crops for as far as the eye could see. He wondered what that might mean for an Amish family.

When they reached the steps to the porch, a young woman appeared in the doorway, a handkerchief tied over her hair. She ran the back of a rubber gloved hand over her forehead. "Can I help you?"

"Yes," Caitlin spoke up first. "We were looking for Mr. and Mrs. Schwartz."

"They're not here." She lowered her hand and narrowed her gaze. "Can I help you?"

"I'm Deputy Caitlin Flagler." The deputy smiled but didn't offer her hand. "And this is my friend Sawyer King. He's a firefighter."

"Oh," the woman said, then her gaze flashed to the spot where the barn once stood, then back to them. "I'm Mary Elizabeth Strand. The Schwartzes hired me to clean out their home.

"Clean out their house?" Sawyer asked. "Are they moving?"

"They already moved to live with one of Mrs. Schwartz's daughters in Pennsylvania."

It wasn't unusual for older parents to move in with their children. Growing up among the Amish, Sawyer knew that many actually lived in smaller homes on the same property. He scratched his head, wondering if they had just run into another brick wall in their investigation.

"I hadn't heard they were moving," Caitlin said. "Did something happen?" She cut him a quick glance, but then focused all her attention on Mary Elizabeth.

The young woman peeled off her rubber gloves and looked down at the worn planks on the large front porch. "I don't like to gossip."

Sawyer and Caitlin both stayed quiet, waiting for the woman to fill the silence.

"I just wanted to make a little extra money so I can help my family."

Caitlin held her hand out to the destroyed barn. "There was another barn fire not far from here?"

Mary Elizabeth nodded without looking up. She dragged

the toe of her scuffed boot along the space between the wood planks.

"We're trying to find out if they're connected. Do you know anything about what happened here?" Sawyer asked.

This time the young woman met his gaze, her brow furrowing. "I thought it was lightning. An act of *Gott.*"

"I suppose it's not impossible, but it does sound a little too coincidental, doesn't it?" Sawyer asked, watching pink blossom on her face.

Mary Elizabeth cleared her throat and squared her shoulders. "Deacon Bontrager says that God is unhappy with us and if we don't repent, there will be more fires."

"Do you know what he meant by that?" Sawyer's scalp tingled, and he and Caitlin once again made brief eye contact.

Mary Elizabeth shrugged. "That *Gott* was unhappy with someone here and punished them by striking down their barn."

"That's a pretty vengeful God."

She shrugged again and Sawyer tried a more direct question. "Why would God be angry at the Schwartzes?" He really hoped his God didn't believe in striking people down. He liked the forgiving version. And from what he knew, the Amish did, too. However, the Amish were humans and sometimes individuals had their own interpretations, and that usually resulted in religion getting messy.

When the woman seemed to be shutting down, Caitlin said, "You're not gossiping. You're helping to save lives, or at the very least property."

Mary Elizabeth looked up and frowned. "It wasn't lightning?"

"We believe this fire and the one at the Sutters were intentional," Sawyer said. "Do you have any idea why someone would start a fire here?"

Mary Elizabeth worked her bottom lip. "I can't believe Mr. and Mrs. Schwartz had to deal with this after losing their grandson in a hunting accident."

Caitlin's eyes flared wide. "Their grandson?"

"*Yah*. It was horrible. I suppose they had to get away. Too many reminders here." She shook her head, as if trying to dispel some horrible memory. "To think the Schwartzes were the only ones willing to take that boy in when he wanted to come home. His own parents shunned him." She made a tsking sound.

"Was their grandson Aaron Miller?" Caitlin asked. The name didn't mean anything to Sawyer.

"*Yah*, poor Aaron." Mary Elizabeth took a step back. "I've probably said too much. I should learn to keep a tighter rein on my tongue. Please, let me get back to work," she added, as if they had made her reveal something better left unsaid.

"Thank you," Caitlin said. "You've been helpful." Something the cleaning lady had said had shaken Caitlin.

The young woman dipped her head, uncertainty in every inch of her posture. She turned and scooted back into the house.

Once they were in his vehicle, Caitlin turned to him. "Do you know the name Aaron Miller?"

"No, I can't say I do."

"He got caught up with the peppers group and he ended up dead in the woods. Everyone first thought it was a tragic accident, but eventually they connected it to the compound."

Sawyer's blood ran cold. "Why did they target him?"

"His friends say he wanted out. Perhaps he was going to talk," Caitlin said. "It was a horrible situation for his entire family. His own parents wouldn't take him back, but his grandparents allowed him to live here while he was trying to untangle himself from that group. Unfortunately, his time ran out before we were able to figure out what that group was up to. The head of the compound had him killed in the woods and tried to make it look like a hunting accident."

A knot twisted in Sawyer's gut. "Is there any way to figure out if my brother was involved with this group?" By the time he came to town, the compound had been emptied and after the initial arrests, the involvement of more individuals was left to speculation. "Maybe someone is targeting families as a warning of some kind. Follow the rules or else."

Squinting her eyes, Caitlin stared out through the windshield. "Let me follow up on something." She grabbed her phone and called someone—from one of the labs, based on the conversation.

He only heard her side of the conversation, but when she was done, he was certain she received the confirmation she needed.

"I must be living my life right because my associate in the lab just finished running some tests. This may not be the news you were hoping for, but the drugs at your cabin were from the same shipment as those confiscated from the preppers compound." She paused a fraction and a soft pink lit her cheeks. "I didn't mean to be insensitive." Caitlin rested her elbow on the doorframe. "I'm passionate about solving cases. Perhaps a little too much so."

Sawyer held up his hand. "You're fine."

"This is definitely another step in finding out what happened to your brother."

"I hope so." Sawyer loved his brother, but Jeb always had a knack for finding trouble. Sawyer cut off the dark thoughts that threatened to take over. He needed to think objectively. Clearly.

"Do you think," Caitlin asked, "that maybe your brother ripped someone off? That now they're getting revenge?" She jerked her thumb toward the scorched earth where the barn once stood. "Their grandson was killed because he was going to rat out the preppers. Again, possible revenge."

Sawyer's eyes flared wide. "Jeb's gone. But Tessa's not. She might be in far more danger than we even realized."

CHAPTER 14

Tessa couldn't stay inside any longer. The walls of her childhood home felt like they were closing in on her. She was bored, but her options on what she could do were limited. So she laced up her boots and set off across the yard, past the men working on the barn, to the field where the neighbors were caring for the horses. She figured if she was in danger, she'd be safe with all the Amish men around. She didn't like to be gawked at, but if they were going to, then at least they could serve a purpose.

"Hey there, Daisy," she said, running a hand down the horse's mane that was hot from the late afternoon sun. "You doing okay?" The horse lifted her head and neighed. "I know, I know…"

She greeted the other horses, and politely smiled yet kept her distance from the men as they came to retrieve their animals for the ride home. When she finally turned back toward the house, she noticed what looked like Deacon Bontrager having an animated conversation—arms swinging, head bobbing—with her *dat.*

"What is that about?" she whispered. Something about the

exchange made her uneasy. Or maybe she was being paranoid after everything she had been through recently.

Ah, but you've come by your paranoia honestly, haven't you? That line of thinking didn't help her growing unease. She wandered back over to Daisy and reassured her that her new home would be ready soon. But something deep down whispered that Tessa might not be around to see it.

Stop! She had to stop being morbid. Wouldn't God protect her?

She made her way across the field just as the deacon took long strides toward his buggy. Relief that he was leaving eased the band around her lungs. She drew in a deep breath and let it out between tight lips.

Joanna appeared on the porch and their father spoke quietly to her. Her sister stomped her foot and their father pointed to the door. No way would his daughter cause a scene at his home.

Oh, no... Tessa's relief had been short-lived. She would have done anything to leave, to get away from all this conflict, but she knew wherever she went, there she'd be.

Heart jackhammering in her ears, she climbed the porch steps. Her father was bracing himself on the railing, staring off into the distance. Tessa felt like a teenager again, awaiting her punishment, the anticipation being the worst part. "What was Mr. Bontrager talking to you about?" She failed at keeping the tremble from her voice, but she couldn't wait any longer.

Her father straightened and turned toward her. A muscle ticked in his jaw under his wiry beard. "The deacon has informed me that his son will no longer be courting Joanna."

Tessa grabbed hold of the railing to steady herself. "Why?" Even before she uttered the question, she knew the answer.

"The deacon doesn't want his son associated with a family who can't keep their children under control."

A mix of anger and shame swept over Tessa, making her hot. "I am not a child."

"You are living in our home." Her father turned to stare out over his property. Perhaps he was too ashamed to look at her. "You asked for forgiveness, yet time and time again, you draw these outsiders to our home." He cut her a hard gaze. "Why do you choose to associate with *Englischers* who obviously don't have enough sense to wear appropriate clothing?"

With her pulse roaring in her ears, Tessa said, "Heather has the right to wear whatever she wants." She wanted to accuse her *dat* of being sexist, but it wouldn't do any good, not when he followed the Amish way. Women were expected to look and act accordingly. Men also had rules to follow. This argument might work on a man in the outside world, but definitely not on her father.

Tessa rushed inside, unwilling to listen to any more of her father's complaints. She found Joanna sitting on the stairs with her face buried in her hands, weeping. Her mother looked up briefly from peeling potatoes but made no effort to console her youngest daughter.

Heart aching, Tessa slid in next to her sister on the hardwood staircase. "I'm sorry."

Joanna looked up, the pain of lost dreams etched in her sad eyes. "What am I going to do?"

Tessa smoothed out a fold on her sister's dress, then patted her knee. "You're a great girl. You'll find someone."

Her sister hiccupped and sniffed.

"Maybe Camp wasn't the boy for you," Tessa suggested, finally admitting what she had suspected all along. "Maybe this is a good thing." As soon as the words came out of her mouth, she realized she had made a huge mistake.

"A good thing?" Her sister's pain had morphed into pure hatred. "A good thing would have been if you never came back. You ruined everything." Joanna grabbed the railing and pulled herself up. She spun on her heel and stomped up the stairs.

Tessa sat there dumbfounded. Every nerve ending vibrated.

Maybe Joanna is right.

Sawyer passed several buggies on his way to Tessa's house. He had rehearsed in his head what he needed to say to convince her to finally let him protect her. Caitlin sat in the passenger seat. She'd be the reinforcements. Perhaps if Tessa refused to come back to the cabin with him, she'd go and stay with a sheriff's deputy. They needed to make sure she was safe until they found the arsonist.

When Sawyer parked on the road in front of the Sutter property, he was relieved to see that the row of buggies was gone. Hopefully that meant all the workers were, too. He found Tessa's father sitting on the porch, chewing on the stem of a tobacco pipe. The tobacco's sweet scent reached his nose when he and Caitlin were still a good twenty, thirty feet away.

Mr. Sutter turned his head slightly and seemed to startle, as if he had been lost in thought and hadn't seen them approaching. The gentleman balanced the pipe on the arm of the chair and slowly stood.

Sawyer couldn't see the man's eyes under the shadow of his brimmed hat, but his penetrating gaze was palpable. "Maybe you should take first crack at this," Sawyer muttered under his breath to Caitlin.

"I'll give it a whirl." Caitlin was in civilian clothes and off duty, but that probably wouldn't matter when it came to the Amish distrust of law enforcement. She quickened her pace to go ahead of him. "Good afternoon, sir," she said. "How are you?"

Mr. Sutter didn't respond; the expression on his face suggested he wasn't sure he would.

"Sorry to bother you." Sawyer spoke up. "We'd like to talk to your daughter."

Mr. Sutter's eyes flashed dark. "*My daughter* has had enough visitors for one day."

Caitlin cut Sawyer a curious gaze, then she turned her attention back to Tessa's father. "We've uncovered some important information. Regarding your daughter's safety."

Mr. Sutter leaned over and grabbed his pipe. "I will keep my daughter safe. Here."

"It's important that we talk to her directly," Caitlin insisted.

"You have no right to come to my home and demand something."

Sawyer scrambled to find another approach, fearful the man would go inside and shut them off completely. They needed to warn Tessa. The time for a wait and see approach had passed.

Mr. Sutter muttered something unintelligible while reaching for the door handle.

"Sir, wait," Sawyer said. "I—we"—he flicked his hand toward the sheriff's deputy—"have reason to believe Tessa was the target when your barn was set on fire."

Mr. Sutter turned slowly around. "This is not new information. As I said, she is safe here."

"I believe she'd be safer if she came with us." His pulse pounded in his head and he mentally willed this stubborn man to relent.

"She can stay with me and my husband," Caitlin said. "We can make sure she's safe until we arrest the person who set your barn on fire."

"No." Mr. Sutter lifted his chin, determination set in his jaw.

"Do you have a gun? Are you willing to use it to protect your family?"

The Amish man blanched at his question. "Surely it will not come to that."

"The fire here wasn't the only one. This shows the arsonist is a very dangerous person. Surely not rational. It'd be safer if she was put into protection. Safer for your entire family."

Mr. Sutter puffed out his chest. "My daughter made a promise to abide by the *Ordnung* and live among the Amish. The bishop will not be as understanding if she leaves again. She has already asked for and received forgiveness."

"They must understand," Caitlin said, pleading now.

But Sawyer knew as well as she that the Amish beliefs often conflicted with theirs. To Tessa's father, she was safe here, among the Amish. *Gott* would protect her. But Sawyer believed you had to use your God-given brain to make the right choices. And staying here as a sitting duck was not an option.

"Good day." Mr. Sutter opened the door, effectively dismissing them.

Sawyer raised his voice and hollered after him, "Will you be able to forgive yourself if something happens to your daughter?"

CHAPTER 15

The sound of raised voices interrupted Tessa's feeble attempts at apologizing to her sister. Joanna's crying had subsided, but she was still giving Tessa the silent treatment, obviously placing all the blame for her failed romance with Camp Bontrager squarely where it belonged.

"I know you don't want to hear this now, but you'll find someone great someday," Tessa said. She wasn't sorry Camp was out of the picture, she was only sorry her sister had gotten hurt.

Joanna muttered something in response, her voice muffled by her pillow where she lay facedown on her bed.

The commotion downstairs seemed to be escalating along with Tessa's anxiety. She peered out the window and her heart dropped when she realized Sawyer was out there arguing with her father. "I'll be back," she said to her heartbroken sister.

Letting her hand skim the railing, Tessa rushed downstairs. Her mother was nowhere to be found. She peered out the window and jerked back when she realized her father was standing by the door. She confirmed what she already knew: *Sawyer.* He was here with the deputy.

She could tell by her father's body language that he was trying to dismiss the visitors. She was debating what she should do when she heard Sawyer say, "Will you be able to forgive yourself if something happens to your daughter?"

Icy-cold fear washed over Tessa. She placed her hand on her belly, wondering how all this stress was affecting her baby.

Her father opened the door and froze when he saw his daughter standing there. "What's going on?" she asked.

"Nothing to concern you," he said.

Tessa grabbed the edge of the door, stopping him from slamming it in Sawyer and Caitlin's faces. "Hold on." She slipped outside. Her gaze slid from Sawyer to Caitlin and back. "What's going on?" She hadn't intended to sound so rude, but she was too afraid to be polite. She was tired of being afraid, too. Afraid of offending her parents, her community. But most of all, she was afraid of not being true to herself in her quest to be a good little rule follower.

None of it was working in her favor. It hadn't been for a long time.

"Is someone going to tell me?" she pressed when they stood gaping at her.

"We learned that another barn fire in Hunters Ridge was at the property belonging to the grandparents of Aaron Miller," Caitlin said.

"The boy who was killed in the woods?" her father asked, genuine concern in his voice for the first time. "That was the fire you mentioned earlier?"

A sick feeling swirled in Tessa's belly. She feared she'd have to excuse herself.

"Yes, sir," Sawyer said. "It's too early to know definitively, but we suspect the two fires might be related."

Before Tessa had a chance to click the pieces in place, her father said, "What does that have to do with my daughter or the terrible fire we've had here?"

There was an apology in Sawyer's gaze. He cleared his throat. "Aaron Miller was involved with the compound. The group they called 'doomsday preppers.' We're worried my brother was involved with the same people. They're dangerous."

Her father turned his gaze on Tessa. "Your husband"—that had to be the first time she had heard her father refer to Jeb as her husband—"was involved with those people?" His face looked crestfallen. "Were you?"

Most of the Amish community were aware of the drug seizures and subsequent arrests on the compound. That her father thought she would get caught up in that kind of activity physically pained her. But had her husband been involved? Did she think *he* was capable? Her entire body began to shake.

"We're trying to find out who set the fires," Caitlin said. "Until then, we'd like to make sure Tessa is safe."

"She'll be safe here," her father said, absolutely convinced of that.

But Tessa couldn't be as confident. And she was beyond tired of bringing trouble to her family's doorstep. "Give me five minutes to grab my things," Tessa said.

"You're not going anywhere. We've already discussed this," her father said, used to having the final say.

Ignoring him, Tessa ran upstairs and threw a few things in a duffel bag.

Joanna pushed herself to a seated position and wiped tears from her eyes. "Where are you going?"

"Someplace else. I might be in danger."

Her little sister furrowed her smooth brow.

Tessa rushed over—before she could overthink it—and

gave her little sister a kiss on the forehead. "I'm sorry I messed things up with Camp for you." She memorized her sister's sweet face. She deserved so much more than that jerk. "But I'm confident you have bigger and better things waiting for you."

Joanna's mouth dropped open, then snapped shut and she turned away from Tessa, as if she had suddenly remembered she was supposed to be mad at her.

"I hope you can forgive me someday," Tessa said as she stuffed the last item into the lone duffel bag and hustled down the stairs.

"Where are you going?" her mother asked, sounding desperate.

Tessa didn't know how much longer she could hold it together. "I have to go. I've done enough damage around here." She brushed a kiss across her mother's cheek. She wanted to ask her to forgive her, too, but she couldn't force the words out of her too-tight throat.

She went outside and found her father walking toward the barn. She peeled her eyes away from him and said to Caitlin and Sawyer, "I'm ready. Let's go."

Tessa stepped through the cabin door for the first time in five months. She had vowed to never come back, yet here she was. She sucked in a breath and tried not to let Sawyer see how being back here had affected her to her very core. It smelled damp and unfamiliar. A building. Not a home.

This place was supposed to be her happily ever after. Her home with Jeb after they got married. Now it was a loose end to tie up. She had thanked Caitlin for her generous offer, but she decided to stay at the cabin instead to take care of a few things before she left Hunters Ridge for good. She had no idea where she was going or how she'd make money, but she'd figure something out.

Please, God, let me figure something out.

"I'm sorry that it has come to this," Sawyer said.

"Not as sorry as I am." Tessa met his gaze, and an intense attraction made butterflies take flight in her belly. She quickly dipped her head as too many emotions crowded in on her. *He's my husband's brother.* She turned and set her duffel bag down on the chair and feigned checking out a few items on a nearby bookshelf. Maybe staying here with Sawyer wasn't such a good idea.

"Are you hungry?" Sawyer opened and closed a few cabinets. "I recently stocked up, so I have soup, eggs, bread. Meat in the freezer. The basics." He turned around and rested his backside against the Formica countertop that Jeb had talked about replacing with granite. Her husband always had big ideas. When she first met him, she loved that he had big dreams. After they married, she worried he was more talk than action. But by then it was too late. She would have never left him.

"No thank you." She forced a smile. She wasn't the least bit hungry, but she'd have to remember to eat for the sake of the baby. Tomorrow.

Sawyer braced his hands behind him on the counter. "Are you sure? I'm not an awful cook if that's what you're worried about. I could whip something up."

"I appreciate that, but I'm really not hungry. Can I take a rain check? Breakfast?"

"Sure. Why don't you get settled in? I certainly don't have to show you where anything is."

She nodded, suddenly overwhelmed with a wave of emotion making her unable to speak.

She picked up her lone duffel bag and slipped into the guest room off the kitchen, the room that probably would have been the baby's room if things had turned out differently. She ran a hand along the quilt on the bed. She had made it for her hope chest when she was a teenager. She had pushed the boundaries by picking the fanciest colors—by Amish standards—of blue, green and a pretty shade of yellow. She had fought to hide her disappointment when Jeb said it was too froufrou for their marriage bed. That was the first of many times she had wondered if she had made a horrible mistake. But she could never admit it. Marrying an outsider was bad enough; divorce was unthinkable.

The quilt was the only personal touch she had made to the cabin filled with furniture and items from her husband's childhood. The excitement of setting up house had quickly been replaced by the reality of being married to someone who seemed moody and dissatisfied.

Determined to shake the ghosts of her past, Tessa changed into comfy sweats and a T-shirt and flopped down on the bed. The smell of something delicious drew her out of her sanctuary. Bent in front of the oven, Sawyer raised an eyebrow at her, and the lone bulb above the rustic island twinkled in his eyes. A half-smile slanted his handsome face and Tessa felt something stir that really shouldn't be stirring.

He straightened and smiled at her. "Do you like brownies?"

"You made brownies?" A warmth bubbled up in her insides.

"Don't be too impressed. It's from a box. I'm a fantastic cook, but a mediocre baker. But hey, Duncan Hines has already perfected the recipe, so why mess with greatness?"

"I suppose not." Tessa slid onto one of the stools that Jeb had picked up at a flea market in town. He had promised her they wouldn't have to take someone else's castoffs once he caught a break. He was always on the verge of catching a break. No matter how often she told him materialistic things didn't matter to her, he wouldn't listen. He seemed to take great pride in providing for her. And he was determined.

So determined that he took to selling drugs? She had been determined to be a good little wife and neglected to ask Jeb more questions.

"Do you really think I'm in imminent danger?" Tessa asked.

"I hate the optics. Aaron Miller—and perhaps Jeb—were involved with the compound. The sheriff's department rounded up the people involved with the drugs, but some may have slipped through. Some sick jerk might be looking to get revenge."

A new wave of fear coursed over her, reminiscent of the night she had escaped the fire. She wanted to ask why someone would want to hurt her. What would it gain them? But in her short life she'd learned people did a lot of things for a lot of different reasons. Not all of them logical.

"Can you keep me safe here? This might be one of the places they'd come looking for me."

"Yes, I can protect you." She took that to mean he had a gun.

She shook her head. "What a mess I've made of my life."

"Don't be so hard on yourself," Sawyer said, his voice filled with compassion. "I know you said you weren't hungry, but maybe a brownie and a movie might be a good distraction."

Tessa smiled. "Sounds good." She wanted nothing more than to get out of her own head.

She settled into the couch with a blanket, even though it was a summer evening. Sawyer placed a plate of brownies, some tortilla chips and what looked like homemade salsa, and two bottles of water on the coffee table. Despite herself, her stomach growled.

"I suppose I'll go savory first, then sweet," she said,

leaning forward to grab a chip and a scoop of the salsa. Some of it plopped on her sweatshirt on its way to her mouth.

Sawyer grabbed a napkin. She held the material away from her body and he gently wiped it up.

"Look at me. I can hardly take care of myself, and I'm having a baby." She laughed at herself.

"You'll be a great mom," Sawyer said, his voice low and husky. Sitting so close, she could smell the clean soap on his skin.

"I hope so." She took the napkin from his hand, feeling self-conscious. She crumpled it up then snagged a brownie, eager for a distraction. "Yum."

"You're easy to impress." Sawyer laughed.

Tessa set the brownie down and turned to face him. "You're a lot different than I thought you were."

"Oh yeah?"

"I don't know if you remember, but I met you before I met your brother." Something flickered in his eyes. He blinked and it disappeared. "You seemed so serious back then. I should have looked beyond the surface."

"I suppose I came off as perhaps a stick-in-the-mud because it had been my job to look after my brother after my mother died. Not a fun job, I might add."

"That's tough. I'm sorry. Jeb told me about that. About how your father bailed and your mother died. That must have been awful." This time the look of pain on his face was unmistakable. She resisted the urge to reach out and brush her hand across his solid jaw. The resemblance to Jeb was unmistakable, yet the angles in Jeb's face struck her as hard, determined. The angles on Sawyer's face were more empathetic. Concerned.

Guilt for even thinking these thoughts unsettled her stomach.

"The first time in my life I didn't feel like I had to watch out for Jeb was after he married you," Sawyer whispered, his voice hushed yet deep. "But I could never fully appreciate it because I was so darn jealous he had gotten to you before I did."

Tessa tucked her chin and placed her hand on her neck, feeling the hot flush of her skin. "I had no idea." And why was he telling her this now? She averted her gaze, feeling uneasy at the turn of their conversation. She forced a laugh, a high-pitched squeak that held little humor. "And look how that turned out."

Sawyer took her hand. "You were not my brother's keeper. Stop blaming yourself for the mess he created."

Tessa slid her hand out from under his. "I should have known better than to marry someone I hardly knew. I'm responsible for that and all the subsequent fallout."

CHAPTER 16

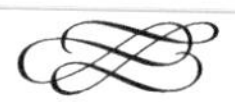

"You have to understand that my brother could never be dissuaded from doing something he was determined to do." Sawyer scoffed and tilted his head, trying to get Tessa to look at him. "Trust me."

"I wish he hadn't gone out that night." There was a faraway quality to her voice.

"Jeb always wanted..." Sawyer was going to say *things he couldn't have,* but he didn't want Tessa to think she had been some sort of prize Jeb had claimed for his own once he knew Sawyer had an interest in her. The brothers had discussed her after meeting her. The brothers had always been competitive. "My brother always aspired to more than our parents had."

"I get that. But we didn't need it all at once." Tessa's voice trembled.

Sawyer's father had grown up Amish and had lamented the dumb system in which he had been raised. He, too, took a job at the local factory and hated the monotony of it. It drove him to drink. He was always looking to blame someone, including his young sons.

"What would you like to do?" Sawyer asked.

Furrowing her brow, Tessa ran a hand across her midsection. "What would I like to do? I…um…"

"I mean, job-wise. Have you ever thought about what you'd like to do in life?"

"Gosh, no. I always thought I'd be a wife. A mom. Like most Amish women. That didn't exactly go as planned." Tessa shrugged, a flicker of something flashed in her eyes. Regret over the path not taken?

"You have your whole life in front of you." He gestured with his chin toward her belly. "This baby is blessed to have you as their mom, but they will just be part of whatever you want out of life. You'll figure it out." He smiled at Tessa and she smiled back timidly. "You're not alone."

"Ha." The sharp laugh was anything but humorous. "I feel very alone." Tessa pressed her lips together and glanced away.

Sawyer itched to pull her into an embrace, but feared he'd spook her. Instead he settled for a promise. "I'll be there for you. Let me know how."

Tessa smoothed a hand across her baby bump. "I appreciate it. I…" Whatever she was going to say, the moment seemed to pass. She cleared her throat. "I thought we were going to watch a movie.

Sawyer scooted to the edge of the couch and grabbed the remote. "What would you like?"

"Anything. You pick."

It took Sawyer several minutes of clicking buttons to get to a streaming service, then through a bunch of movies he didn't think his guest would like. "How about this one?" He held his hand up, ready to hit play on a newer action movie.

Tessa reached out and touched his hand, lowering the remote. "Do you really believe Jeb was dealing?" The look in her eyes—a mix between *please no* and *please be truthful*—hurt his heart. When he didn't immediately answer, she bit her bottom lip. "You think I'm naive."

"I think you love my brother and want to believe the best of him."

"We had grown apart by the time he disappeared."

A jolt shocked Sawyer's system and he found himself holding his breath.

"I'm not sure I ever loved him. *Really* loved him." She slumped and covered her face with her hands. She wept quietly, and he sat there frozen, unsure of how to comfort her. She swiped at her cheeks and asked, "Does that make me an awful person?"

"I don't think anyone would ever call you an awful person. You're human."

"I think I was caught up in the idea of him." She started to explain something he didn't expect—or require—an explanation for. "I wanted desperately to get out of my parents' home. Jeb was fun. He pursued me." She paused, her lips trembling as she fought to hold it together. "It felt good to be pursued."

"You don't owe me an explanation," Sawyer said. "I need to find out what happened to my brother, sell this place, and then we both can get on with our lives." Whatever that looked like.

She seemed to take in every square inch of the cabin with her watery eyes. "You don't plan on staying in Hunters Ridge?"

"No." The single word came out quicker than he had intended, but was he being completely honest? A lot depended on her. "I suppose I have a lot to consider..." He held up his hand to indicate the baby.

"You don't have any responsibility when it comes to the baby." Her brows drew together. "Not at all. Besides, my family wants me to give the baby to my brother to raise."

Shock jolted his system. "Are you?"

Tessa kept her gaze averted and cradled her belly. "I could get a fresh start. Move to another Amish community and pretend none of this happened."

"But it did." Sawyer kept his voice calm despite his pulse roaring in his ears. "There are other options." He covered her hand with his, the baby underneath. "You don't have to do that if you don't want to." He couldn't begin to imagine the impossible choice she had.

Her eyes narrowed; a spark of anger shot in his direction. "What other options? I'm poorly equipped to be a single mother."

"You're resourceful. Besides, as my brother's wife, you're entitled to half the proceeds of this cabin. Maybe I..."

He struggled to gather his thoughts. There was no way she could hand her baby off. Could he sit by while his brother's child was given to an Amish family to raise? Could he take in the child? How would that be any different than giving the child to her brother? Actually, it would be worse: he didn't have a family. He wasn't Amish. Man, he didn't know if raising the child Amish was important to her.

"Oh no, this cabin belongs to you and Jeb," Tessa said. Neither of them touched on the fact that they didn't know if Jeb was alive or dead.

"Don't dismiss the idea so quickly," he cautioned. "You're a smart lady."

She dragged a long strand of hair out of her face and tucked it behind her ear. "Based on my life choices, many could question how smart I am."

"You're young. You've had some tough breaks. I promise I'll help you."

"Don't make promises you can't keep." The defeat in her voice suggested she still didn't trust him.

"Give me a chance."

They locked gazes and held it for a beat too long. He wished she could see what he saw, but he had said too much already. He needed to allow Tessa Sutter to make her own plans.

One of the King brothers had already derailed her life. He wasn't about to do it to her, too. She needed to figure out her future without him breathing down her neck.

CHAPTER 17

Tessa and Sawyer spent the next few days cleaning the cabin and organizing all the stuff. In the evenings they watched movies and played cards. She didn't want to admit she was growing very fond of Sawyer. He was all the things she had hoped her husband could be, or become, but time had run out for them. She'd never admit it out loud, but she was glad they had a lot of work to do because it bought her time to figure things out. And to spend with Sawyer.

Growing up Amish and without a lot of materialistic things, she had never seen so much "stuff." When she and Jeb lived here, she had never bothered with the attic or all the storage spaces tucked away behind the walls. Goodness, she didn't even know most of them existed. She had always assumed various mechanical systems were tucked behind the tiny doors. Despite the quantity of items to sort, she was happy to have something to keep her busy as she weighed all her options that agreeing to take half the proceeds from the sale of the cabin afforded.

Could she honestly accept the money? Could she afford not to?

When she came to stuff she and Jeb had brought into the home, she tried to pack with efficiency and without sentimentality. The latter would have made her a weepy mess. And she wanted to be strong. She also didn't want to consider Jeb's reaction when he turned back up and discovered she had sold their home and run away with half the money.

Do you really believe he's alive?

She and Sawyer had been at this for a few days when lunchtime rolled around. Tessa didn't realize how hungry she was until Sawyer set out a plate with chicken salad sandwiches on the most delicious bread she'd ever tasted. *Who is this man?* His brother liked to be served. Be the man of the house. And Tessa didn't necessarily mind because she had grown up with that model of a relationship. Her mother served her father. Her father worked the farm. Made the money. It all seemed like that was how the world was supposed to work.

Until it didn't and she was left without a husband and a means to support herself. And then she met this man who liked to cook and care for her.

"I keep ruminating about me and my big mouth." Tessa finally gave voice to the words that had been haunting her. Why had she told him she never loved his brother? "Jeb was —is—" Her voice faltered. "A good person." Their conversation had run the gamut, but his brother—her husband—had inevitably come up. Why had she been so honest about her relationship with Jeb? She hadn't shared her concerns with anyone before Sawyer. It'd seemed pointless. She'd never get divorced. "Jeb wouldn't have done anything intentionally to hurt me."

"Stop beating yourself up. I'm glad you're comfortable

confiding in me. You've been under intense pressure, and I'm sure it's more challenging because you haven't had anyone to talk to."

"So true. My parents want me to forget my past and move on. What will happen if I give my baby to my brother and his wife? Do they grow up thinking I'm the aunt? How would that even work? How would that feel?"

"Did you talk to your parents about this?" Sawyer asked. "Maybe there's another way."

"I tried to talk to my mom. She said we'd have to talk to my father. My father reminds me that the bishop has been gracious in allowing me to come back, considering all my 'sins.'" She used air quotes over the word sins because, in her heart of hearts, she'd never consider her legal marriage and the conception of this baby to be a sin. This little guy—or girl—was meant to come into this world. The baby was a blessing.

For you or your brother's family?

Tessa leaned back and placed her hand on her belly, thinking about it, but still not knowing the answer. Despite—or maybe because—her father and the bishop decided everything for her, she felt so unsettled. And she wasn't sure where she stood now that she had left again. She could only imagine the rumors about her staying here with a man who wasn't her husband. A new flush of embarrassment was about to roll over her when the baby kicked. The heat of shame was replaced by joy. "Oh, oh, he's kicking." She sat upright, prcssing her palm to her belly.

Sawyer smiled. "A he?"

"Yeah, I think it's a boy." Tessa reached out and took Sawyer's hand. "Want to feel your nephew's kick?"

He tilted his head, as if to say, *Are you sure?* She smiled and took his hand and guided it to her belly. As if taking requests, the little guy gave his uncle a solid kick.

Light radiated in Sawyer's eyes. "Oh, definitely a boy. He's a strong one."

"Are you saying a girl can't be strong?"

He laughed again. "You just told me you thought it was a boy. Don't bait me."

"Ah, you're so easy to bait."

They locked gazes for a long moment, then she turned away and scooted to the front of the couch, his hand falling from her belly. She pressed on the arm of the couch and stood.

Her face was on fire. "I suppose I better get back to work."

"Tessa," Sawyer said and she turned around. "I didn't mean to make you feel uncomfortable. It's okay."

She waved her hand in dismissal. Perhaps this cabin was too small for the both of them.

CHAPTER 18

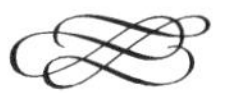

Sawyer secured the box of books, using the last bit of packaging tape. He set the empty dispenser down on the shelf and ran the back of his hand across his forehead. Despite having all the windows open, it was stifling in the cabin.

Tessa was sitting at the kitchen table with a stack of papers overflowing a shoe box. He joined her and watched over her shoulder. A black-and-white photo of him and his brother standing in front of the cabin poked out from under an old fuel bill.

"May I?" he asked, reaching over and picking up the photo. Both he and his brother had dirty faces, their clothes too small, their feet bare. "You'd think we grew up in the sixties, but my mom was in a photography phase, trying black-and-white film before digital became commonplace."

"I found this box in the back of the guest room closet."

He slid into the chair next to hers. "Mind if I look with you?"

"Of course. I'd love some context." She flipped over a

photo. "It seems your mother entered a few of these photos in contests."

The idea of his mother having a passion like photography was foreign to him. Then a long-ago argument came to mind. His father was complaining about all the money she spent on film and developing. The photos seemed to stop when he was about ten. The idea bummed him out. He pushed the box to the center of the table. "You up for a walk?"

"Yes," Tessa said, with more enthusiasm than he had expected. She plucked at her T-shirt. "It's so stinking hot in here."

Sawyer held out his hand. "Let's go, then. Do you have hiking boots?"

"How far are we going? I have tennis shoes."

"They'll do. Hurry up and change. Meet me outside."

Once outside, he led her down the path toward the creek, the same path he had followed more times than he could count.

"It's so peaceful out here," she said. Some of the strain from her face disappeared in the fresh air.

"It is." They continued to walk in companionable silence. When they reached the creek where his brother's snowmobile had been found submerged, he turned to look at her. She had gone pale, apparently thinking about the accident. "Are you okay?"

Tessa nodded slowly. "I haven't been here since last summer, before...well, Jeb." She lifted a hand to tent her eyes. "I can't imagine what he was thinking, cutting across the ice."

"The deputy suspects he was being chased. Did you hear anything that night?"

"They asked me all these questions." Her gaze stayed trained on the opposite shore. "I heard his snowmobile when he left and then I thought I heard another one. I wasn't sure if he came back to grab something or if someone met him at the house. It wasn't unusual. I mean, not in the middle of the night, but sometimes for early morning deliveries they'd needed a few extra guys. They might meet here or down by the bridge. Once the snow arrived, they were excited to ride their snowmobiles." She twisted her lips. "You know how guilty it makes me feel that he might have been in trouble and I didn't even get out of bed to look out the window."

"You have to stop doing that to yourself. You are not my brother's keeper." Sawyer was debating the wisdom of bringing her here.

She shrugged, apparently not convinced.

"I've hiked these woods countless times." He studied her face. Her messy bun, her shorts and T-shirts reminded him of the teenager he had first laid eyes on around the bonfire all those years ago. But now her features were more mature. More worldly. More thoughtful.

Apparently sensing his scrutiny, she turned and looked at him. "You've been searching for him." It wasn't really a question, but he felt compelled to answer.

"Yes. I haven't stopped looking. At first, I was convinced he had been injured and was wandering these woods disoriented. Too much time has passed..." He left that thought unfinished. Either way, his brother needed to come home.

Tessa's lips twitched. "I've gone to bed every night with that image in my head." Her voice shook. "The thought of him freezing to death haunts me. The search teams canvassed this whole area for weeks before giving up."

"I know. But maybe they missed something. I have a map and mark off the locations I've searched."

Tessa squinted up at him. "Do you really think he's out here?"

Sawyer understood what she meant without saying it. Not him, but his body. "I don't know. I really don't."

"Eddie was his closest friend and claimed he knows nothing." Tessa cleared her throat. "And according to him, Jeb lied about having a delivery that night." She sighed heavily. "I've spent the past several months alternating between mourning Jeb and being angry at him." She bent down and picked up a rock. She tossed it in the water and the two of them stared at the ripples.

Sawyer placed his hand on the small of her back and she surprised him by leaning into him. What he wouldn't have done to have swept this woman off her feet before his brother did.

"You want to keep going?" Sawyer asked, afraid to stay there holding her. Afraid of what he might confess.

"Sure." There was a distant quality to her voice.

"We'll head a bit north, then into the woods beyond where I last searched." He swatted at a bug flying around his head. "Let me know when you're tired."

Tessa laughed. "I'm always tired. So I'll tell you when I'm ready to go."

"Sounds good." He held out his hand and she walked ahead of him.

Sawyer prayed every night that they'd find his brother, but he also didn't want to be the one to find his body. And if he thought he'd really stumble upon it, he wouldn't have brought Tessa.

CHAPTER 19

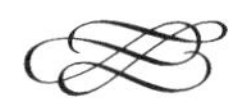

Tessa took a cool shower after their sweaty, buggy, itchy hike through the woods. She hadn't really thought they'd find Jeb, and she suspected Sawyer felt the same way. He needed to feel like he was doing something. *Anything.* Sawyer had turned out to be someone she could really care about. And she wasn't sure that was a good thing.

Jeb had painted him as a domineering pain in the backside, a killjoy, and self-centered. Sawyer was none of those things. She had gotten to know both men, yet the brothers didn't seem to know each other, not really. How sad, considering the opportunity might have passed.

After the refreshing shower, Tessa dressed in soft shorts and a T-shirt and sat crossed-legged on the couch, expecting to spend her evening hunkered down in front of the TV. That had become their routine. She wasn't sure where Sawyer had disappeared to. She spread a blanket across her bare legs and picked up the remote. Watching TV was a new pastime for her and she had come to realize she enjoyed the mindlessness of it. She flipped through the stations until her eyes grew heavy.

She wasn't sure how long she had been dozing when she felt something brush her arm. She blinked open her eyes and found Sawyer sitting on the coffee table, staring back at her with a look in his eyes she was afraid to explore. His hair was wet from the shower and he smelled good, really good, like aloe and Dove soap.

"Hey, sleepyhead," he said. His husky voice did something to her insides, not that she'd ever admit it.

Suddenly really hot, she pushed off the blanket and sat up. She could think better this way. "I guess the hike knocked me out. I've gotten lazy. My parents have had me hiding inside at the farm, and well…it's easy to get lazy."

"Give yourself a break. You're expecting." He smiled. "You must be hungry." He tilted his head toward a plate on the coffee table next to him. She hadn't even heard him in the kitchen. "I had some leftover pasta. It tastes better the second day."

She leaned over and grabbed the bowl, suddenly realizing how hungry she was. "A girl could get used to this." Another wave of heat infused her cheeks. "That sounded a little bold."

"Bold isn't a bad thing." The twinkle in his eye made her like him even more.

No, no, no.

"Not if you're Amish. Subdued and obedient are far better qualities."

"I suppose it depends on who you ask." The intensity of his gaze sent a wave of pinpricks across her flesh.

She shifted to the edge of the couch and stood. She took her pasta bowl and went into the kitchen. She had to put some distance between her confused feelings and that hot man sitting on the coffee table. Maybe pregnancy had jumbled her hormones and her emotions. And most definitely, her thinking. She glanced back toward the family room. He was easy on the eyes and even easier company.

Ugh.

She slid onto a stool and twirled the pasta onto her fork. Despite trying to focus on her food, she found herself watching Sawyer plop down in the spot she had just vacated and flip through the channels. How can there be so many channels and nothing to watch?

A knocking sounded at the door and Sawyer set the remote down and glanced over his shoulder. "Are you expecting anyone?"

"No." She swallowed the food in her mouth and it felt like a lump sliding down her dry throat. Alarm made the hairs on the back of her neck prickle to life. The past few days had been so peaceful she had almost forgotten about the potential danger she might be in.

Sawyer got up and grabbed the gun out of the end table drawer. "Stay there." Sawyer held out his open palm to her. "Out of sight." He held the gun down by his thigh as he answered the door.

"Hello," a woman said, "I'm looking for Tessa."

It took a heartbeat for Tessa to recognize Heather's voice. She rushed toward the door and touched Sawyer's back, aware of his solid muscles under his dark blue T-shirt—despite her best efforts to remind herself that she was still technically married. To his brother. "It's Heather," Tessa said, her breath loud in her ears. "It's okay."

Heather smiled. "You're one hard person to find."

Tessa slipped in front of Sawyer, completely aware of the heat radiating off his body on the warm summer evening. "Hi, Heather."

Heather tilted her head, her thin hair brushing her sun-kissed shoulders. "Uh, aren't you going to invite me in?"

Tessa stepped back and bumped into Sawyer's chest. She looked up at him and his gaze was fixed on the woman at the door. "Excuse me," Tessa said, "please come in. How did you know I was here?"

Heather stepped into the heavily shadowed cabin and took everything in like a looky-loo at an open house. "Your little sister told me you'd come back here." Her gaze dropped to the gun in Sawyer's hand. "Is that on account of me?" She gave him an exaggerated frown and held up her hands. "I'm not a threat. Trust me."

"Can't be too careful," Sawyer said, not bothering to crack a smile. He took the gun with him to the kitchen on the other side of the open room and got himself something to drink. Then he slipped out the back door.

Tessa wasn't sure why she felt the need to apologize to Heather, but she did. "We're still on edge because of the barn fire." She omitted the part about the Schwartz barn fire possibly being connected.

Heather whispered, "So it's 'we' now?" She raised her eyebrows. "What's going on with you two?"

"No, no, nothing. Goodness." Tessa felt like she was protesting too much.

"Okay, then." Heather raised an eyebrow, clearly enjoying herself. Then, perhaps sensing Tessa's discomfort, she grew somber and placed her hand on Tessa's. "Sorry, I'm just teasing. But I wouldn't blame you. He's even better-looking than Jeb."

Tessa held up her hand, the thin gold band on her ring finger. "I'm married."

"Jeb's not here," Heather joked, then clamped her hand over her mouth. "Oh goodness, I really stepped in it. Please don't listen to me."

"It's okay." Tessa smiled cheerily, always feeling the need to put others at ease. But hadn't she been thinking the same thing about Sawyer? She could hardly fault her friend.

Is that what Heather is? A friend? No, she was more an

acquaintance. Eddie's girlfriend. Tessa didn't have many people she could call friends. Her Amish friends were mostly married with children and could hardly associate with her now. She had been too smitten with Jeb to allow herself to find friends outside her marriage.

"Can I get you something to drink?" Tessa asked, remembering her manners.

Heather waved her off. "No, no, I've been thinking of you since I came over to the farm…and your situation."

Tessa raised her eyebrows as if to say, *Oh.* In her current life, she had several "situations" going on.

"My sister had her third baby two years ago and she's getting rid of all her stuff—crib, bouncy chair, onesies. All the stuff that adds up. Having a child is expensive. So I figured you might want some of it."

Ah, the pregnancy situation.

Tessa tilted her head. "Oh wow, I could use all the help I can get." Did that mean she had decided to keep the baby? Raise him herself instead of sending the child to grow up in her brother's perfectly nice Amish family? No one could fault her for changing her mind. She had agreed under duress. She drew in a deep breath, keeping her spiraling thoughts to herself.

"My sister is looking to clear everything out, so if you want anything, we'll have to check it out soon."

"Okay, sounds good."

"Are you back here for good?" Heather asked, looking around the cabin.

"I don't think so. Sawyer plans to sell this place. I'll figure it out." Tessa felt so naive when people asked her questions like this. Most adults had plans, goals, money. She was tired of flying by the seat of her pants.

"I have an extra bedroom," Heather said, snapping her gaze back to Tessa, her expression indicating the idea had come as much of a surprise to her as anyone. "Just until you get your feet on the ground, I mean. It's nothing fancy. It might be fun having a roommate." Heather seemed to really be warming up to the idea. "If it makes you feel better, you can pay me a small rent. Whatever you can afford."

"I don't know."

"Come on," Heather said again. "I live close to town. You can walk to the stores. You'll have some independence. And then whenever you get your feet on the ground, you can go. Sound good? I can take you to see it after we pick up the baby supplies from my sister."

Just then, Sawyer walked back into the cabin. His gaze landed on Tessa and a half-smile hooked his lips. A jolt of attraction shot through her. The pregnant wife of someone else had no business feeling this way about this man.

Tessa turned back to Heather. "Could we go bright and early tomorrow morning?"

CHAPTER 20

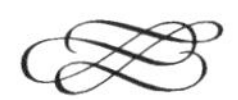

"You ready to go?" Sawyer rapped softly on the open bedroom door. He was going to drop Tessa off at Heather's apartment in town on his way into the fire station. He wasn't thrilled about leaving her side, but figured this wasn't a bad alternative, perhaps better than leaving her here alone at the remote cabin.

"Ready as I'll ever be." Tessa turned away from the full-length mirror and frowned, tugging at a T-shirt that stretched across her growing belly. "Maybe Heather's sister has some maternity clothes, too." She rolled her eyes and laughed in a self-deprecating way.

"We can go shopping. You don't have to take someone else's hand-me-downs." Sawyer had grown up poor and had worn more than his share of previously worn clothes. He'd hated it.

"Beggars can't be choosers," she said, twirling her hair up into a long ponytail, exposing the pale skin of her neck. "Really, I'm not proud. If her sister is going to get rid of it, I'm happy to accept it."

"I hear ya," he said noncommittally. In his heart, he knew

that Tessa had the right attitude. It was difficult to change preconceived notions formed as a kid, especially when his classmates had made fun of his too-small or too-worn clothes. Kids had a knack for homing in on someone's weakness and then picking at it until a kid wanted to explode. Perhaps their childhood had been tougher on his brother. Maybe that was why Jeb was suspected of doing whatever it took—even if it was illegal—to make sure the cycle didn't continue.

Tessa stuffed her feet into her sneakers, smooshing their backs with the heels of her feet.

He smiled. "Want a hand?"

She tilted her head as if trying to decide something, her long, silky ponytail flowing over one shoulder. She plopped down on the edge of the bed, seemingly resigned to her predicament. "Sure. Bending over makes me want to puke."

"Do you need something else to eat? Maybe that will settle your stomach." Sawyer crouched down in front of her and eased his finger around the back of her shoe, then the other.

"It'll pass."

Sawyer tied her sneakers, and when he was done he looked up at her. "I used to have to do this for Jeb. I swear he was a teenager before he figured out how to tie his shoes."

Tessa laughed, a genuine laugh. "He was probably playing you. He always preferred when I did things for him."

Sawyer patted her knee and then stood up. "That sounds like my brother."

The mood in the air suddenly shifted. Sawyer offered his hand to help her stand. It felt delicate in his. She stood easily, but he didn't let go.

He ran his thumb across the back of her hand and whispered, "I wish..."

He shook his head, stopping himself. He had no right to wish for these things.

"I wish a lot of things, too." Tessa dipped her head. Electricity shot through their touch, amplified by the long pause. It was Tessa who finally pulled her hand away from his and cleared her throat. "Let's get moving or you'll be late for work." Her voice sounded artificially cheery.

He hated that he had made her feel awkward.

Once they were in his truck headed into town, Sawyer felt compelled to clarify the details. "Heather said Eddie was out of town, right? I don't have a good feeling about him."

"Yes, I asked her about him. I think he had some deliveries to Buffalo. It'll just be me and Heather. Her sister's husband ended up dropping all the baby items to her apartment. We'll sort through them." She let out a long breath, then placed her hand on the console between them. "I'll be fine."

"And you grabbed the cell phone I gave you? I programmed it with my number. Call me if you need *anything.*" He had picked up a disposable cell the last time he had been in town. After giving it to Tessa, he hadn't seen her with it once. He wished he had that much discipline when it came to his phone.

"Got it." She patted the small purse in her lap. "Please stop worrying about me. You're making me nervous." She wasn't the only one, but he kept that thought to himself.

Sawyer pulled into a small apartment complex that had probably been built in the seventies when they had hoped manufacturing and workers would flock to the small town. Instead, the Amish had found the farmland less expensive than in neighboring Ohio and had made the trek east around the same time. As a result, the apartments in town ended up being underutilized. From the looks of the empty parking lot, not all the units were occupied.

"Text me when you're done and I'll pick you up," Sawyer said, still debating if this was a good idea. But in the end, it wasn't up to him.

"Are you sure? I can walk to the fire station."

It was only a short walk into the center of town, but he'd feel better if he came and got her. "I can scoot out. The only issue I'll have is if there's a fire."

"Murphy's Law, right?" Tessa said.

"Hush." The station had been relatively quiet—a few medical calls and a fender bender—since the fire that could have killed Tessa.

While they were still in the truck, the door to one of the lower units opened and Heather appeared. She gave them a friendly wave and jogged over. Tessa climbed out and then leaned back in the doorframe. "I'll call you as soon as we're done."

Apparently overhearing the conversation, Heather said, "I can bring her home. Really, it's no bother. I thought maybe we'd grab lunch or something." She shrugged, waiting for his approval.

Tessa smiled reassuringly at Sawyer. "I'll let you know what we're doing."

"Take care." Sawyer watched as the two women disappeared into the apartment. Out of habit, he scanned the area. There wasn't any sign of anyone else. The sun poked through the swaying tree branches, creating moving shadows on the cracked asphalt. This was the first time Tessa was out of his sight in days and he had a bad feeling about it.

Once inside, the cloying smell of cigarette smoke reached Tessa's nose. *Does Heather smoke?* She hadn't detected the telltale signs of tobacco use on Heather or her clothing. Perhaps it was from previous company.

Eddie...

Tessa froze, indecision making her knees weak.

"Go on in," Heather said as she closed the door. The thunk of the deadbolt hitting home sent a wave of pinpricks coursing across Tessa's arms.

With more than a little trepidation, Tessa walked down the narrow hallway that opened to a small kitchen on the left and a living room straight ahead. Maybe she was just paranoid after all the events of the past year. She forced herself to remain in the moment.

Focus. Don't panic.

Panels were missing from the venetian blinds covering a sliding glass window on the back wall. The carpet was threadbare in spots. The couch cushions were worn. Would Tessa really want to live here with her baby?

"How long have you lived here?" Tessa asked, trying hard to imagine bringing a baby home to this place. A yellow water stain marred the popcorn ceiling. A swatch of flower wallpaper curled off the wall. One of the tiles under her feet was loose. Who was she to judge? She was here due to this woman's generosity.

Heather lifted a shoulder. "Since I was eighteen and moved away from home." She seemed to take in the place through Tessa's eyes. "I've been saving money and won't have to live here much longer."

"That's right, babe." Eddie stepped out from a back hallway and wrapped his arm around Heather's shoulders in a possessive manner.

The woman subtly recoiled, but Tessa noticed it and it made her knees go weak. A strained smile slanted Heather's narrow face. She blinked up at her boyfriend. Tessa's heart dropped at the exchange.

"I thought—" Tessa pressed her lips together. *No, don't give anything away.* This felt very much like a trap. Her heart thundered in her chest and her hand went protectively to her baby bump.

"Go on…what did you think?" Eddie asked, his voice gravelly. His eyes didn't leave Tessa's face.

Alarm chugged through Tessa's veins. She forced a smile that she hoped didn't look as fake as Heather's. Her mind raced. "Oh, I didn't realize you'd be here today. I'm sure we could do this another time. When it's more convenient." She found herself glancing over her shoulder at the locked door, then back to Eddie. "I should go." She spun on her heel to leave.

Eddie's hand came out and grabbed her wrist and twisted. She bit back a yelp. "You're not going anywhere."

"Eddie, babe," Heather pleaded. "You said—"

"Shut up!" A vein bulged in Eddie's forehead. He released Tessa and smacked Heather across the face.

The poor woman let out a surprised and pathetic "Oh!" as if she was afraid her shock would unleash more violence.

Tessa gasped. Heather held her cheek and averted her gaze, looking ashamed and guilty. Very, very guilty. *Oh, what have you done*? Tessa's legs felt wooden. Could she make it to the door and out before he grabbed her again? Could she risk him hitting her? The baby?

"Sit down and shut up," he said to Heather, his lip curling up, giving his face an even more menacing appearance with his short brush cut and neck tattoo. Then he turned to Tessa and drew her tightly to him in an awkward side hug. A hint of body odor emanated from his sweaty skin.

She fought her gag reflex. Every inch of her wanted to run outside, feel the soft breeze on her skin. Inhale the fresh air. She wanted to rewind the day and stay home.

With Sawyer.

A new wave of nausea made her even more desperate to get out of this situation. She swallowed down a sickly, sweet taste in her mouth. "I don't feel well." She wasn't hopeful that this would win her any sympathy points, but she had to try. At least if she tossed her cookies at his feet, he couldn't say she hadn't warned him.

"Let me get you some water?" Heather was obviously asking Eddie for permission.

"Take her to the bedroom," Eddie said evenly. "She can rest there."

"No." Tessa touched her purse. "I can walk into town." She could call Sawyer as soon as she got out of here.

Eddie reached into his breast pocket and tapped out a cigarette. He took his time lighting it, then took a long drag. He blew the smoke into Tessa's face. The look of pleasure on his curved lips made icy dread pool in her stomach. He was sadistic. There'd be no convincing him. But she had to try.

"Please. Stop. I need to go."

Eddie sucked his teeth. "What are you worried about? My mom smoked when she was pregnant with me and I turned out fine." He placed too much emphasis on the word *fine,* considering how he had ultimately turned out. His laugh dissolved into a hacking cough. He pounded his chest with his fist.

Apparently not waiting for her boyfriend to give her the green light, Heather rushed to the kitchen and returned with a glass of water. "Here."

Tessa took a small sip of the tepid water that had a foul taste. Her hand trembled.

"Take her to the guest room," Eddie pressed, a hard edge to his voice. "I'm not going to tell you again."

Heather gently took Tessa's elbow and guided her down the long hallway. "I'm so, so sorry," she whispered, terror making her voice tremble.

"What's going on?" Tessa asked urgently. Heather was her only hope.

"Do what he says and you'll be fine. Okay?" Tessa tripped and Heather steadied her. "You'll be fine."

"I feel sick." Tessa should have never come here.

"Do what he says." Heather repeated, as if she was terrified to go off script. She glanced over her shoulder, then pushed open a door at the end of the hall, revealing a dark, musty bedroom. *Is this the bedroom Heather was going to try to sell Tessa?* No, that had all been part of a ruse to get her here.

Stupid. Stupid. Stupid.

A surge of adrenaline made Tessa panicky. "Don't leave me in here."

"Please do what he says, okay?" Heather repeated the familiar refrain, sounding like she wanted to cry.

Eddie appeared in the doorway and Heather startled back from Tessa, as if she had been caught doing something wrong. He leaned his shoulder on the doorframe and crossed his arms. "I'll make this easy on you. You want to get out of here? Tell me where the money is."

"What money? I don't know what you're talking about." A gathering darkness tunneled her vision. *The drug money.* Her first instinct had been to lie. Had she only dug herself in deeper?

Don't pass out.

Don't pass out.

"That's garbage. Your family's barn burns down and you're rebuilding almost immediately. That costs money." His voice grew louder. "I want my share."

"The Amish community helps each other when someone's in need." She pressed her shaky hands to her chest. "I personally don't have any money."

"Yes, you do."

Tessa cut her gaze to Heather. "Please. Tell him I don't

have anything. That you brought me here to pick up baby clothes from your sister. Why would I take hand-me-downs for my baby if I had money to buy new things?"

Heather didn't budge and a horrible realization slammed into Tessa. There were no baby clothes. Of course there weren't. Another trick to get her here.

Eddie fisted his hands, a look of barely concealed rage on his face. "Jeb stole from our last shipment of drugs. The people he stole it from found out. Thought I was in on it. Jeb's such an idiot. I had to convince them I'd make things right."

Make things right? Perspiration prickled Tessa's skin. "I don't have anything." The sheriff's department had it, but she couldn't tell him that. Could she?

Think. Think. Think.

Eddie hovered over her, his stale breath making her stomach heave. "I brought Jeb into the business, then he stole from me." He scoffed. "Fool thought he could get away with it."

The room began to spin.

All the deliveries.

The extra money they suddenly had for things.

"Please. Jeb's gone. You'll have to wait for him to come back. You can ask him. This has to be a misunderstanding. You're friends." Tessa's words sounded delusional even to her. Jeb had been gone for nearly half a year. He wasn't coming back. Tears clogged the back of her nose.

Eddie started giggling and couldn't stop like a deranged villain in one of those creepy movies she and Sawyer caught on Netflix. "You're a fool." He jerked his chin at Heather who was cowering in the corner. "Go get it. Show her."

Heather scampered out of the room like a little girl afraid to disobey her father. She returned with a small wooden box, something Tessa might have found in her parents' home. Something most likely crafted by the Amish.

"Open it," he said, amusement lacing his tone. "Show her."

Heather opened the box, revealing a man's gold wedding band. As if moving on someone else's volition, Tessa picked up the ring and turned it over in her fingers, feeling the weight of Eddie's stare on her. She squinted at the inscription, but she already knew. It was the date she and Jeb got married at the courthouse. Reflexively she glanced at her left hand, the gold glinting in the limited light from the hallway. They vowed they'd never remove their rings.

"How did you get this?" Tessa asked.

"He suffered the consequences."

Adrenaline surged through her veins as she fisted her husband's ring. "Where is he?"

Eddie tilted his head and a smarmy smile slanted his thin lips. "He's not coming back."

A crushing weight on her chest made it hard to breathe. Tears filled her eyes and the entire room went out of focus. "Why isn't he coming back?" Her tiny voice squeaked, when she wanted to scream. Rage. But she had nothing left in her.

Across the room, Heather sobbed.

"Shut up!" Eddie yelled, his voice vibrating with fury. "I had to kill him. It was his own fault." He jammed his hand through his unkempt hair repeatedly. "He was a liability. He ruined everything by skimming from our shipment. Consider yourself lucky that you weren't killed. The people he stole from aren't forgiving. And I need to pay them back."

"The drug dealers at the former compound?"

Eddie tapped his nose. "Not much gets by you, darling." The condescension in his tone was palpable.

"Aren't they all in jail?" Tessa couldn't wrap her head around this.

"Jeb started skimming before the compound was raided.

Not everyone was arrested. A few of those guys came looking for the drugs."

"The night Jeb disappeared?"

"I offered him up," Eddie said, seeming pleased with himself. "Him or me."

"He got a text that night and he bolted," Tessa said, trying to put the pieces together.

Eddie cut his gaze to Heather and she took a step back, as if he just now realized something. "You—" Eddie called her every name in the book. "You're useless. You warned him, didn't you?"

Tessa swallowed her nausea. She should have kept her thoughts to herself. Now she feared for Heather's life. The young woman had tried to warn Jeb.

"He was your friend," Heather whispered. "How could you turn on him?"

"You have to put your nose into everything." He clamped the back of her neck and forced her head down. "You idiot."

Tessa's hands flew to her mouth. "Why did you have to kill him?" Her voice cracked. "He still would have told you where the stuff was," she quickly added. Her purse slid off her shoulder and hit the ground. She had given up trying to convince Eddie he was wrong.

"The jerk went out onto the ice. He pawed his way out of the frigid water." There wasn't a shred of emotion behind his blank stare. "I was waiting for him on the opposite bank."

Tessa hugged herself and shuddered, imagining the man she had once loved fighting for his life after plunging into the icy water only to meet his fate at the hands of a friend. "You..." Her jaw began to tremble as she tried to process his confession. She reached down for her purse and Eddie kicked it away. She stepped back and put her hands in front of her belly protectively.

"Leave it there," he demanded, as if he were training a

puppy. "I gave him a chance to come clean. He claimed he hadn't done anything. He kept up the lie. I planned to force him back to the cabin to get the drugs..." A shadow crossed the depths of his eyes with something akin to regret, maybe. "Then they got impatient. Made me kill him on the spot to prove my loyalty."

Made him? A single tear tracked down her face.

"A few of us went back the next morning to search for ourselves. I suppose it's a good thing you weren't home."

Her mind raced through the events of the first days after her husband disappeared. "I thought someone had been in the house. I thought I was just tired and..." She couldn't even put her emotions into words.

Eddie crouched down in front of her. "He thought he could steal from a group like that and not pay the price? He had to be an example and they made me do it. It would give them something to hold over my head. A guilty person doesn't call the sheriff." He dragged his hand across his short hair. "A few guys from the compound lost their patience. You don't get nine lives in this business." Eddie straightened and punched the wall. "Now tell me where the drugs and money are."

"The sheriff's department has them," Tessa whispered, finally revealing what Sawyer had found in the secret compartment in the main closet.

Eddie whirled around and got into her face. "You're lying. You're desperate and you need the money. Why would you hand them over? You're not stupid." His hand snaked out and he clutched her neck and squeezed just like he had done to Heather. "You've got a baby to provide for." His words sounded like they were coming through a long tunnel as stars danced in her line of sight.

"Stop! Stop!" Heather cried. "She's telling the truth."

Eddie released Tessa and glared at Heather. "What do you know?"

"She came here for old baby clothes. Why would she do that if she had money? Right? Right?" Heather's tone got more desperate as the story gained traction. "She told you that."

"I promise you." Tessa rubbed her neck and coughed. "I don't have the money. I don't have *any* money."

Eddie jammed his fingers into his greasy hair repeatedly. "Call your boyfriend. If you're telling the truth and the sheriff's department has it, he can get it back."

"Jeb's brother is a firefighter. He wouldn't have access to something the sheriff's department has," Tessa said, praying if Eddie thought there were no more angles to pursue, he'd set her free.

The deranged look in his eyes said otherwise. Her heart sank.

More likely, he'd kill her.

Like he had killed Jeb.

CHAPTER 21

Sawyer finished some paperwork then checked the time. He had expected Tessa to text him by now. He didn't have any missed texts or calls. Maybe her lunch with Heather had run long.

The fire alarm sounded and Sawyer jumped to his feet. So much for obsessing about where Tessa was. "Hey," he said to Elijah, a young Amish kid who prepared meals at the fire hall, "if a woman comes in here looking for me, tell her we're on a call." His gaze drifted to the street, willing Tessa to appear. "Ask her to stay here until I come back, okay?"

Elijah gave him a mock salute. "Will do."

"Come on!" his captain called, urging Sawyer to action. He suited up and jumped on the fire engine.

When they arrived at the call, a barn was fully engulfed.

"Not another one," one of his fellow firefighters muttered.

Sawyer took in the scene. This location was closer to town, with neighbors on either side. "If it's our arsonist, he's getting bolder."

Broad daylight. Neighbors. Definitely not a good sign.

As a few of the firefighters rushed to unfold the hose,

Sawyer ran up to the house where an Amish teen stood on the porch. "Anyone inside the barn?"

"*Neh*," he responded, staring at the blaze, concern etched on his young face.

"Animals?" Sawyer asked.

He shook his head. "My car." The defeat in those two words said it all. But Sawyer didn't share his concern. Material things could be replaced. Lives couldn't.

"Did you call it in? See anything?" Sawyer asked. If the Amish kid had a car, he probably had a cell phone.

"Yeah, I was playing video games when I got up to get a snack and saw the flames shooting out of the barn." His wide eyes gave him a bit of a vacant look. "I ran out with a bucket, but it was out of control."

"Where is the rest of your family?"

"Visiting my grandparents." He folded his arms over his chest and rolled up on the balls of his bare feet. "I didn't feel like going." Sawyer suspected this kid usually had an attitude but the fire had destroyed that, too.

"Okay, then. Stay here on the porch where it's safe. Someone from the sheriff's department will want to talk to you. Don't go far." Sawyer spun on his heel and jogged back to the fire-fighting efforts.

After the barn was reduced to charred wood and smoldering embers, Sawyer was walking the perimeter looking for a cause when a neighbor ran over.

"Hey," the man said, dressed in dirty jeans and a ripped T-shirt. He didn't give off an Amish vibe. "I came home to feed my dog at lunchtime and saw all the fire trucks over here. What in the world happened?"

"We're looking for the cause." Sawyer was used to gawkers. Give them the information they needed and most were on their way, or at least they stepped back. "Have you seen anything out of the ordinary around here? Strangers, maybe?" Sawyer studied the man's face searching for any tells that he might know more than he's letting on.

"Not at all. An Amish family lives here," the man said, fumbling with his phone.

Sawyer tried to hide his annoyance. He wasn't in the mood for rubberneckers looking to take a cool video to post online. Another suspicious barn fire didn't do anything for his nerves, nor did the fact that he still hadn't heard from Tessa. "Sir, if you'd step back..." Sawyer said, trying to hide his frustration.

"Hold on." The man held up his phone, insistent. "I have one of those security systems on my house. I checked it when I got home. Because of the fire, you know. I think it caught someone setting the barn on fire."

Sawyer blinked, not sure if he heard him correctly and immediately feeling contrite for snapping at the man. "Can I take a look?"

The two men stepped under the shade of a nearby tree to get a better view of the small screen on the cell phone. Sure enough, someone in a broad-brimmed hat and brown pants and a white shirt lit something and then launched it onto the roof.

Sawyer slid the bar on the bottom of the screen and rewatched the video, studying the image closer. *Hard to tell.* "Do you recognize them?"

"Kind of hard to see his face in this video," he said. "But" —he tapped his fingernail on the screen—"he's young. He doesn't have a beard." A beard was a mark of a married man among the Amish. A man who had a wandering eye couldn't pretend he wasn't married unless he risked explaining to his wife why he had shaved off his beard.

"Any other footage?" Sawyer asked. His pulse chugged in his ears. Amish. The arsonist was definitely Amish—or at least dressed plainly. This was the first solid lead.

"I can scroll through it. I wanted to get over here right away and show someone this," the man said. Clearly this was the most exciting thing that had happened to him in a very long time.

Sawyer looked up and saw Caitlin cutting across the yard. "You have to see this. Mr.…"

"Jimmy Ernst," the neighbor said, offering his name. "Lived here in Hunters Ridge my whole life. Long before the Amish came here. My father used to farm this land. Me, I'm not much for growing things. I have a job in maintenance at the cheese factory."

"What do you have, Jimmy?" Caitlin asked, apparently already familiar with the guy.

Jimmy explained what he had found on his security footage. Caitlin tilted her head toward his house. "Want to load this up on your home computer? I'll come over myself or one of the other deputies will."

Jimmy nodded, clearly happy to be part of the investigation. "Um, I have to get back to work at the factory. Can we do this later?"

"Maybe I can call in to your boss. Explain the situation. You've been very helpful."

Jimmy smiled widely, apparently jazzed to be a part of the investigation. "Sounds good to me." He turned and jogged toward his house, seeming eager to see what else his security camera had picked up and probably pumped he didn't have to report for the second half of his shift.

"That's a fantastic break," Caitlin said. "The arsonist has gotten bold. He must have known the family was away but hadn't counted on the son staying behind. Or the neighbor's camera." The deputy was clearly pleased. "I'll follow up with Jimmy. You do your thing here."

"Will do. Thanks."

Sawyer turned back toward the charred remains of the

barn. He quickly checked his phone and his dread grew when he realized Tessa still hadn't texted him.

"Hey, Caitlin," he hollered. Sawyer jogged across the yard to catch up with her. "Can you do me a favor?"

Caitlin tilted her head as if to say, *Sure, what?*

"Can you see if one of the deputies could take a swing by a location? I haven't heard from Tessa and I should have by now. I'm getting worried."

"Sure. Give me the address. I'll call one of the guys on patrol to do a welfare check."

"Thanks." Sawyer was going out of his skin, but he had a job to do here and no real reason to suspect Tessa was in danger. Heather had offered her baby clothes. Harmless stuff. Right?

Locked in the guest bedroom, Tessa sat on the bed with her back pressed against the wall, taking shallow breaths to control her panic and nausea.

It worked. Barely. Perhaps the idea of getting sick in these tight quarters and then not being able to get away from the smell kept her from throwing up.

Don't think about it. In through the nose. Out through the mouth.

The raised voices of Eddie and Heather reached Tessa through the hollow bedroom door. Even though Heather was most likely pleading her case for letting Tessa go, Tessa wasn't feeling very charitable toward the person who had lured her here under false pretenses. The young woman might have had a change of heart, but some good that did Tessa now. Surely Heather knew her boyfriend well enough to suspect some half scheme could easily go sideways, especially when she already knew he had killed Jeb. Perhaps it was the promise of money that made Heather cooperate with her boyfriend. Or maybe his abuse had warped her thinking.

Tears prickled the back of Tessa's nose. Her husband was dead. She had feared that from the beginning. But suspecting and knowing were different. Very different.

Don't focus on that. Breathe.

A loud rapping sounded on the front door.

Someone's at the house!

Hope propelled Tessa off the bed. She flattened her hands against the bedroom door and strained to listen. Heather and Eddie's arguing immediately ceased. Tessa held her breath. Deep voices. A man. More talking but she couldn't make out the words.

Should I make noise? Let them know I'm here. What if it's someone who'll hurt me? Or the baby?

She froze with indecision. Over her pulse pounding in her ears, she heard the door click closed. A car engine started. Tessa couldn't see who it was because the exterior window was boarded up.

If I had a chance, I missed it.

"Leave her alone," Heather shouted. "Stop, stop, stop!" The shrieking raked across Tessa's brain as it got closer and closer.

Eddie was coming for her. Tessa backed up against the wall with nowhere to go.

The bedroom door slammed open and the doorknob crashed against the wall. She moved as far away from him as possible, but that was as far as she could go. It was futile.

Eddie charged her. His hand went immediately to her neck again. "What did you do? What did you do?" Spittle flew from his lips and rage darkened his eyes.

Tessa clawed at his wrists. He was too strong. "Nothing," she croaked. "Please. Let. Go."

Something passed over his face and he dropped his hands

and sagged. A yellow light cut across her crumpled bed and his wild eyes bounced around the room. "Where is it? Tell me now."

"What?" Tessa asked, holding her hand to her neck in a defensive posture.

"The cell phone."

Tessa pointed to the hall. "In my purse. Out there."

Heather disappeared, then returned a moment later with Tessa's purse. Eddie dumped out its contents. The phone hit the floor and skittered under the bed.

Realizing she couldn't have made any calls, he grabbed her wrist and pulled her down the hallway. "Lock up," he said to Heather. "We're taking our friend someplace no one can find her."

CHAPTER 22

Sawyer strode over to the fire captain's SUV. All the trucks had already returned to the station and Sawyer was still wrapping up his preliminary investigation on scene. The physical evidence supported arson. The video images were a godsend. He just hoped there were better images that could identify this guy.

The captain was on the phone. Sawyer grabbed a cold bottle of water out of a cooler in the back seat, then leaned against the truck, waiting for a ride back to the station.

Deputy Flagler burst out of the neighbor's house and jogged over to him. "Glad I caught you."

"Yeah," Sawyer said, "is there better video of the arsonist?"

"Yes, yes, we'll get to that. But I needed to tell you that Deputy Kimble stopped by Heather's apartment."

Sawyer pushed off the bumper of the SUV. She had his full attention. "Was Tessa there?"

Caitlin shook her head. "A man answered. An Eddie Ward."

Adrenaline surged through Sawyer's veins. He tossed his

coat into the captain's SUV and turned back to Caitlin. "We've got to check on Tessa. Heather specifically said Eddie was out of town."

"Eddie was the man your brother was supposed to meet up with the night he disappeared, right? That's why I'm concerned."

"According to Tessa, but Eddie denied it. Still, it doesn't look good. Come on, can we take your patrol car?"

"Let's go."

The drive to Heather's apartment where he had dropped off Tessa a few hours ago was the longest drive of his life. He tried her cell phone over and over, but it went straight to voicemail. Sawyer focused on the yellow divider line on the road, unable to process all the emotions assaulting him.

He had one job.

One.

Protect Tessa.

And he had failed.

Don't go there. You don't know that. Not yet.

Caitlin's patrol car bucked over the uneven entrance to the apartment parking lot. "There!" Sawyer pointed. "That unit."

The deputy barely had time to slam the vehicle into park and Sawyer was out running, holding his gun down by his thigh. Thankfully, he had grabbed his concealed weapon. He lifted his free hand and pounded the door. It vibrated in its frame. He twisted the knob and the door popped open. He ignored Caitlin's shouts to "Hold up."

He didn't care if he was breaking the law. He had to find Tessa.

The air in the closed-up apartment smelled musky and reeked of tobacco. The place wasn't exactly tidy and it was hard to tell if there had been a disturbance.

Sawyer raced down the back hallway, his gun up and ready. His pulse roaring in his ears. The last door yawned open, revealing a sparsely decorated bedroom. The window boarded up.

He flipped the light switch in the room. *Click. Click. Click.* Nothing. He backed up and turned on the hall light. The yellow light streamed into the room.

That was when he saw it: Tessa's purse. He scooped it up and looked inside. Her phone. The screen displayed all his missed calls.

He sensed Caitlin in the doorway. He spun around and she was holstering her gun. "You're not very good at taking commands, are you?" She arched one eyebrow, then jerked her chin in his direction. "What did you find?"

He held up the purse and phone. "Tessa's." Panic rose in his throat. He should have never dropped her off here.

Caitlin held up her hand. "We'll find her. Where would be a logical place to take her?"

Sawyer jammed his fists on his hips and looked around. "I can think of a few. The cabin? The woods?" He cursed under his breath.

"Before we go off half-cocked, let's do a quick search of this place. Look for mail, an address, anything that might lead to another place for them to hole up."

"Yeah, yeah," Sawyer said distractedly as he rushed through the house, opening and closing drawers and closets.

It was when he got to the bathroom and opened the medicine cabinet that he found it. A note with one word scratched on it with today's date.

Cabin.

"I told you everything has been cleared out of the storage places," Tessa said when Eddie planted his hand on the small of her back and pushed her into the cabin. Tessa sent up a silent prayer that Sawyer would find his way back here soon. He had to be wondering about her.

"You could be lying. Now you're going to show me exactly where you found the money and drugs Jeb stole. Otherwise we're going to wreck this entire place."

Tessa met Heather's gaze for a fraction of a moment before her so-called benefactor glanced down. The woman had made countless pleas to Eddie to "Let it go," but her boyfriend was determined. Tessa tried not to think how Eddie's confession about killing her husband didn't bode well for her. For either of them. He wouldn't just let her go, would he? He'd have to kill her too if he wanted his secret safe.

She let out a long, slow breath.

"Whatcha so nervous about?" Eddie leaned in close and she found herself holding her breath. "Show me what I want and everything will be a-okay."

Tessa took Eddie to the closet in the bedroom she once shared with Jeb. She opened it and got down on her knees and felt for a small release in the floor panel and the door popped open. She reached in and patted the space. "See. Empty."

Eddie spun around and pointed at Heather. "Check it out."

Tessa backed out and Heather got down on her hands and knees and leaned into the cubby. "I don't see or feel anything, Eddie." She sat back on her heels and pressed her palms together. Her face was blotchy from crying. "Please, let's go. Tessa had nothing to do with Jeb stealing those drugs. She's innocent in all this."

"Innocent!" Eddie exploded. "It's always a stupid woman who ruins everything. Jeb and I were best friend since high school. We had a good thing going until *she* came along."

The room swayed under Tessa's feet.

"He got big, stupid ideas. He ruined everything."

Out of the corner of her eye, she saw a patrol car pull up outside the cabin. Realizing she'd never get a second chance at the element of surprise, Tessa spun around and bolted for the bedroom door. Eddie's fingers raked her back, leaving a trail of shivers, but he was unable to grab hold.

She kept running.

A loud crash sounded behind her. When she reached the exterior door, she glanced over her shoulder. Eddie was scrambling to his feet. He must have tripped.

Mouth having gone dry, she yanked open the door and burst out and landed in Sawyer's arms. "Thank God you're here. We have to go. He's coming. He's coming."

Sawyer wrapped his arm around Tessa and pulled her behind him. *Thank you, God! Tessa's okay.* Trembling, but okay. He hadn't discovered how much he cared for her until he realized he might really lose her.

Okay, focus. He kept his eye trained on the open door behind them. "Okay, okay, run to the patrol car." When she didn't move, he said, more firmly, "Now!"

She nodded, then took off running. She stumbled over a root from one of the large maples but recovered without going down. Once she was out of sight on the other side of the patrol car, he stood on his porch. Jeb and Tessa's porch, and his parents' porch before that. The air had a completely different energy.

Caitlin said something to Tessa, most likely along the lines of, "Stay behind the vehicle and keep your head down." The deputy then ran in a crouched position and joined him on the opposite side of the door. "I'd tell you we'll wait for backup, but I have a feeling you won't listen," she deadpanned.

He lifted an eyebrow. "We can't wait. Eddie is in there with his girlfriend. Who knows what his frame of mind is." He stated the facts, trying not to think about what this all meant for his little brother.

Caitlin cursed under her breath. "I hope we're not looking at a hostage situation."

"Me, too." He tilted his head toward the door. "Let's take him."

The sheriff's deputy opened her mouth to protest a firefighter making the calls in this situation, but this was his house. He decided to do it and ask permission later. He prayed he didn't get either of them killed.

They walked into the house, alert and ready to take down any threat. Sawyer gestured with his head toward his closed bedroom door. They took cover on either side of the door.

Caitlin shouted out commands for Eddie to come out. When he didn't, she lifted her hand to count to five, then they both stormed into the room.

Eddie held his gun to Heather's head while she was on her knees weeping. "Please, Eddie," she sobbed.

"It's all over. Put the gun down," the deputy said, aiming her weapon squarely on Eddie.

Eddie turned his anguished face toward Sawyer. "I didn't want to kill him. They made me." He slumped his shoulders and that was when Sawyer took his chance.

He dove at his brother's best friend from childhood, sending his thin frame crashing backward. Eddie landed on the hardwood floor and his gun went flying out of his hand.

Eddie didn't even try to get up. Caitlin rushed in and handcuffed him and yanked him to his feet.

As she read him his rights, Sawyer tended to a sobbing Heather. "Are you okay?"

The young woman nodded, sniffling. "Thank you."

As he led her outside, he said, "You were the one who left the note that you were headed to the cabin, weren't you?"

"Yes." Heather burst out crying. "I couldn't stop him. He told me he wanted information from Tessa." She bowed her head and cried harder. "I'm such an idiot. I thought if he got what he wanted, he'd leave her alone."

"Stop being so hard on yourself," Sawyer said. "In the end, you did a good thing." He smiled. "Tessa is going to be okay because of you."

"What's going to happen to Eddie?" Heather asked.

"Prison." He hoped. He caught sight of Tessa walking slowly in their direction. An overwhelming relief pumped through his veins.

Heather laughed and hiccupped at the same time. "Stupid question, I guess." She ran her hand under her nose. "What's going to happen to me?"

"I don't know. But maybe the courts will go easy on you, all things considered," Sawyer said.

"Thank you for helping me," Tessa said, her voice thick with emotion. It seemed that both Sawyer and Tessa were willing to forgive Heather for the role she played in getting Tessa to show up at the apartment. The woman was obviously under Eddie's control.

Heather shrugged, a silent tear trickling down her face.

Caitlin tucked Eddie into the back of her patrol car, then returned and pulled Heather aside.

Tessa turned to Sawyer. "Eddie admitted to killing your brother." Tears welled in her eyes.

Sawyer pulled her into an embrace and swallowed

around a knot of emotion. Sadly, this did not come as a surprise, but it was hard to hear. His goof-ball brother was dead.

"I'm so, so sorry," Tessa said, crying into his shoulder.

"I'm sorry for you, too." Sawyer's voice was thick with emotion as he ran his hand down the back of her head.

After a moment of consoling each other, Tessa stepped out of his arms and swiped at her cheeks. "It's over, isn't it?" She seemed almost shell shocked.

Sawyer brushed a strand of hair from her face. "It's over." He studied her closely. "Are you okay? The baby?"

Tessa placed a hand on her belly. "Got the fright of my life, but we're okay. Thanks to you."

"I would tell you that I'd send another vehicle over to pick you up, but well…you're already home," Caitlin said, interrupting the moment. *Probably just as well.* "I have to call another deputy to pick up Heather. You'll also need to give statements. Both of you."

Sawyer held out his hand. "Thanks for everything, deputy." Then he turned his attention to his brother's wife. *His widow.*

"Yes, thank you," Tessa said. "I'm truly grateful."

"You're one strong woman," Caitlin said. "I'll be in touch." She turned and waited with Heather by her patrol car.

Sawyer nodded. "Hey, one more thing. Any word on the fire today? Any more images?"

Caitlin held up her index finger. "Yes, they got some clear images. Just verifying his identity."

"Another fire?" Tessa asked, sounding absolutely exhausted.

Sawyer explained the circumstances of the brazen daytime arson.

"Do you have the photos? Maybe I'll recognize him since I grew up in the Amish community," Tessa said.

Caitlin scrolled through her phone then held it up.

What little color Tessa had in her cheeks drained, leaving her a pasty white. "That's Camp Bontrager. He had been courting my little sister until he decided she wasn't good enough." She sighed heavily. "Because of me."

CHAPTER 23

Tessa's knees went weak and she felt Sawyer tighten his grip around her waist. "Camp set the fires?" Her voice sounded high-pitched and squeaky in her ears.

"The *Englisch* neighbor had cameras and caught him in the act."

Tessa dipped her head and ran her hand over her forehead. "What an idiot." Heat crept up her neck and face at the irony. "His entire family is keen on enforcing the rules." She shrugged. "Maybe he thought he had to punish those who weren't following the *Ordnung*." She looked up at Sawyer. "Do you know if the family—the one with the fire—if they had any ties to the compound?"

"No idea. But the kid who was home told me he had a car inside the barn."

Tessa took a deep breath, then ran her hand over her ponytail. "That's against the *Ordnung*." She shook her head again. "This is all so unbelievable."

Sawyer guided her with a hand on her back. "Let's go in. Get out of this heat. You don't look so good."

Tessa bit her lower lip. "I don't know if I can stay here. I need some time." Too many memories, the least of which was being kidnapped and forced to prove she didn't have drugs hidden somewhere in the cabin she once shared with her husband.

Jeb was gone. *Really* gone.

Sawyer nodded. "I can put you in a hotel."

How could she tell him she didn't want to be alone without sounding desperate?

"You know," Caitlin said, "you can stay at my place on Bird's Nest. Austin just finished renovating it. We kept some of the better-made furniture from the previous owner. So there's a bed and somewhere to sit."

"Oh, I couldn't."

"Please, no worries. It's sitting empty. You're welcome to stay there as long as you want." She tilted her head and smiled in the easy way she had about her. "If you stay there long enough, I might ask you to show it to prospective buyers." She waved her hand. "But that's a problem for another day. "Why don't you head there and I'll stop by later and we'll get all these reports done."

Tessa furrowed her brow. "Are you going to arrest Camp?"

"I'm calling it in right now."

"How about that ride after all?" Sawyer asked. "I'd like to pick up my truck from the fire hall."

"Sure thing." Caitlin reached out and brushed Tessa's arm. "Just take it easy. Everything is okay now."

Caitlin turned and walked away and Tessa leaned into Sawyer, allowing the stress of the past several months to roll off her. She reached down and squeezed his hand. "Thank you for rescuing me."

~

Sawyer got Tessa settled into Caitlin and Austin's "flip house." They sat on the couch with pizza and chips. Five minutes into a movie, Tessa's steady breathing indicated she was asleep. She had her head on his shoulder.

He could get used to this.

He still hadn't processed that his brother was dead. There were so many open items, but for now he knew Tessa was safe. And he knew what had happened to his brother.

A little after eight, a quiet knock sounded on the door. He carefully moved Tessa and put a pillow under her head. An epic fight scene played out on the small screen.

He could see Deputy Caitlin Flagler in her civilian clothes through the window. A man was standing behind her. Sawyer unlocked the door. "Hey."

"Sorry to show up so late, but I figured we should get your statements while your memories are fresh." Caitlin furrowed her brow. "Where's Tessa?"

Sawyer glanced toward the living room. The back of the couch blocked the view of Tessa. "Sleeping on the couch."

Caitlin drew up her shoulder and smiled. "Oh, sorry. She must be exhausted." Then, without waiting for a reply, she pointed her thumb at the man behind her. "This is my husband and jack-of-all-trades, Austin Grayson. When I told him you guys would be staying here, he wanted to check on a few things." She slanted them a smile. "He's a perfectionist that way."

Sawyer reached out and the two men shook hands. "Nice to meet you. Thanks for letting Tessa stay here. She's had a bit of a rough go."

Austin jutted out his lower lip. "You're not staying here, too?"

"I…um…" Sawyer shook his head, not often finding himself without words.

Caitlin rolled her eyes. "He's afraid of the rumor mill."

She walked past him and turned the lock on the window over the sink in case he had missed it. "You have to get over that. You know where you stand on things."

"Tessa needs her space."

"Actually, I'd feel a lot better if you stayed here." Tessa stood next to the couch, her ponytail mussed from sleep. She smiled at Austin and blinked slowly. "So this is the infamous husband of our favorite deputy."

Austin tilted his head. "Who doesn't love a gun and a badge?"

"Don't let him kid you. He was FBI before he gave it all up to move here with me," Caitlin said.

Austin planted a kiss on the top of his wife's head. "She thinks it was a sacrifice. Ha. Now I get to fix houses on my own terms with no boss. I love working with my hands. I get to see the fruits of my labor."

"No boss?" Caitlin laughed.

"I mean, you're my only boss." He playfully chucked her arm, barely making contact.

"Got that right." The smile stayed on Caitlin's face when she turned back to Tessa. "He's still trying to get me to take his last name, but I enjoy letting the townsfolk wonder about us." She laughed. "Ready to give a statement?"

"Sure." And Tessa relayed everything that had happened.

When they were almost done, Tessa asked, "Did they arrest Camp Bontrager?"

The deputy nodded.

"I don't imagine he or his family took it lightly."

"No, the sheriff was worried that they were going to have a riot. Turns out the entire Bontrager family are a bunch of zealots. We took the father and all five sons down to the station. One of our detectives will sort it out."

"Camp had been at my house earlier," Tessa said.

"Earlier? Today?"

"No, no, the day of the fire. He came by my house probably three hours before the fire started." Tessa shuddered at the memory.

"We'll make a note of that. Listen…" Caitlin put her hand on Tessa's forearm. "Get a good night's sleep and we can talk again tomorrow."

Tessa nodded.

Austin pointed at Sawyer. "Give me five minutes and I'll give you a tour of all the mechanicals and stuff, in case you have any issues."

"Sure. Thanks."

After getting some instructions, he and Tessa saw Caitlin and Austin out.

Tessa turned to him. "I didn't mean to put you on the spot by asking you to stay." She shrugged. "I'm still a little freaked out."

"It's not a problem. I don't mind." He reached out and tucked a strand of hair behind her ear. "You want to finish the movie?" He smiled and Tessa laughed.

"Can we start it over? I think I missed the beginning."

"You think?" He took a chance and leaned over and pressed a kiss to the top of her head. "I'm glad you want me to stay."

"Me, too." She pressed her cheek into his chest and they stood that way a long time. Just holding each other. Comforting. Innocent.

They had both been through a lot, but neither of them was quite ready to face the future.

Whenever that might be.

CHAPTER 24

hree months later

"Well, we did it," Sawyer said, squeezing Tessa's hand. "Mr. and Mrs. Sawyer King." He held the door to the Hunters Ridge courthouse and ushered her outside. The sun of the gorgeous early fall day sparkled in her eyes. He couldn't remember the last time he had been this happy.

"I never thought I'd have a shotgun wedding," Tessa said, running a hand over her expanding belly. She had picked up a pretty pink flowy dress at a boutique on one of their trips into Buffalo. "Now what?" She waggled her eyebrows at Sawyer and swung around to plant a kiss on his lips, her baby belly bumping into him.

They had been living apart for the past couple months. She had been living at Caitlin and Austin's fixer-upper while he had moved back to the cabin. With all the guilty parties arrested, she had finally felt safe enough to live on her own.

But now that she and Sawyer had fallen in love, it was time to take the next step. It was a series of events he couldn't have foreseen, but here they were on their wedding day.

"Hmmm...." Sawyer playfully patted her behind.

Tessa giggled and swiped at his offending hand. "Stop, people will see."

"Let them talk," he said. He was done worrying about what people would say about him marrying his brother's widow. They were in love. And in a way, he felt a purpose in taking care of her and the baby. But mostly, he loved her for her.

He had loved her since the first time he had seen her at the bonfire when they were teenagers. He hadn't had the nerve to speak to her first. Jeb had been the more adventurous one.

Sawyer wasn't willing to lose Tessa a second time.

She slipped her hand into his and they walked toward their car. "I hope that wasn't too anticlimactic for you." They had decided to have a simple ceremony with only the officials as witnesses.

Sawyer stopped her and turned her around to face him. He leaned down and kissed her. He'd never grow tired of her soft lips, her curves, her warm smile. He whispered into her lips. "I really, really don't care who sees."

Sawyer opened the car door for her, then jogged around the other side and hopped in. They had made a reservation at a cute bed-and-breakfast on the edge of town for their wedding night. But first he had a surprise for her.

Tessa sat in the passenger seat, more content than she had felt in a while.

Sawyer leaned over and placed his hand on her knee. "Are you tired?"

She drew in a deep breath and let it out. "I'm at peace." That was something she honestly never thought she'd be able to say after the night Jeb disappeared. It had been a whirlwind since this summer. As part of his plea deal, Eddie had led the sheriff's department to Jeb's body. She and Sawyer had been able to give him a proper burial. And for Heather's part in all this, she had been given probation. Despite any bad she might have done, Tessa was grateful to her for saving her when it really counted.

As tough as it initially was, they had gotten on with their lives. And knowing how fragile life was, they didn't want to waste another minute moving on with the future.

Their future.

"I've heard good things about this B&B." She stared out the windshield as they climbed the driveway up to the old, converted farmhouse. She furrowed her brow at all the cars parked on the lawn out back. "The owner warned me they were hosting an event this afternoon but assured me it would be over earlier."

Sawyer cut her a sideways glance and a handsome smile slanted his mouth and warmed her heart. She couldn't believe she was married to this man and that her baby would have this wonderful man as their father.

Sawyer parked in an open spot marked for *Overnight Guests*. He climbed out and opened the door for her. They walked inside hand in hand.

The din of a party reached them when they walked through the front door. "Hello," Sawyer said to a young woman behind the desk. "Sawyer King and this is my wife, Tessa. We have a reservation."

The woman looked up and an uncertainty flitted across

her face, then her eyes widened, as if she had remembered something. "Mrs. Lapp has to check you in. If you don't mind, you can find her in the back room, through there."

Sawyer nodded and tilted his head in the direction the woman had pointed. "Come on."

Tessa held back for a fraction of a second, suddenly realizing she might be walking in on something. Sawyer leaned in close. He smelled of clean aftershave and aloe. She'd never tire of that smell.

"It'll be okay," he said reassuringly.

Sawyer reached out and opened the French doors. A celebratory "Congratulations!" rose up from the crowd.

Tessa's hand flew to her chest. "Oh my." She looked up at Sawyer. "I thought we agreed to no wedding reception." Despite what she said, she couldn't keep the smile from her face.

"We did agree. And I always keep a promise."

Before he had a chance to say anything more, Caitlin, dressed in a pretty purple dress with a lacy sweater, rushed up to them with a cake with a baby on it. "Welcome to your baby shower."

Tessa laughed and gently punched her husband. "You!"

"A promise is a promise. You said nothing about a baby shower. The people who love you wanted to do this for you."

Tessa glanced around the room to see her sister Joanna, her brother's wife, who'd come to understand Tessa wanted to raise her own child, and her cousin, who Tessa had helped with her babies. Between the pretty fall dresses and the plain Amish garb, it made for an eclectic vibe. And Tessa loved it. These were the people who had made her who she was today.

Joanna rushed up to her and handed her big sister a beautifully wrapped gift. "Open it."

Tessa took it and looked around. Was she supposed to do

this now? Ah, she couldn't turn her sister down. She seemed so happy. Tessa unwrapped the box and pulled out a beautiful crocheted blanket. "Sweetie, I love it."

"It's beautiful," Sawyer said. "You're very talented."

"It's green. Since we don't know if it's a boy or girl."

Tessa pulled her sister into a hug. "I love it."

Joanna slipped away from her grasp, blushing. The sisters had rarely shown such affection for each other. Her little sister tilted her head and studied the floor.

"What is it?" Tessa asked.

Joanna stepped closer and lowered her voice. "I was a spoiled brat about Camp. I thought you ruined everything." She sighed. "But it turns out you saved me a lot of heartache."

Tessa's heart warmed. "I'm glad to hear that. I only want the best for you."

Camp and his self-righteous family had turned out to be worse than she thought. Currently, only Camp was facing charges for exacting his own kind of justice on those he felt weren't following the Amish way. But Tessa wouldn't be surprised if his brothers were eventually implicated.

"I know you love me." Joanna waved her hand. "We don't need to talk about that now. Come in. I made cookies." She lowered her voice. "And Mem made her potato salad."

Tessa glanced around the room, looking for her mother. She saw several of Sawyer's friends from the fire hall. A few of the contractors from the house. Some of the employees at the library where Tessa had recently been hired. *A job!*

"But of course, Dat didn't think it was a good idea for her to come."

Tessa smiled tightly, trying not to let the reminder that she wouldn't be fully in her family's life ruin this day. She was simply glad her sister had found a way to share in her celebration.

Joanna led her and Sawyer to a place of honor

surrounded by a stack of gifts. Tessa sat and Joanna knelt in front of her and handed her the first package. Tessa accepted it and placed her hand on the wrapping paper. She paused and took everything in. Absorbing every detail of that moment. Her new, wonderful life.

Sawyer reached out and covered her hand and whispered, "Is everything okay?"

She took his hand and brought it to her lips. "Everything is perfect. Absolutely perfect."

Hope Baker stuffed the last tablecloth into the sack and tossed it over her shoulder. "Oof," she grunted as the heavy bag landed solidly on her back. Rolling her shoulders, she peeked through the slit in the door leading to the large dining room/living room combination. The guest of honor's husband carried the last of their haul out the door. He seemed like a good man. Hope prayed he was, for his new wife's sake. Hope had found out the hard way that a person didn't always know another person's heart until it was too late. From what Hope overheard—she didn't like to think of herself as the type of person who would eavesdrop, but she was still trying to figure things out in Hunters Ridge, and a person got a lot of information from lingering in the background and keeping her ears open—this mother-to-be had already had her share of heartache.

Hope tried not to feel bad about listening to all the gossip. She had been the subject of it more times than she cared to count and it made her skin crawl, especially because a lot of it was mean, hurtful…untrue. She had escaped the worst of it, managing to arrive in town a month ago, land this job, and pretty much stay under the radar.

"You don't have to go to the laundromat now. It's late."

Hope spun around to find Mrs. Lapp standing in the kitchen behind her. *Mary.* Hope adjusted the handle of the bag slung over her shoulder. "I don't mind." She figured she'd have the place to herself.

"Save it until Monday." Tomorrow was Sunday and her Amish boss would be keeping the sabbath. The laundromat would be closed, as would most other stores in the small town.

"I'd rather get it done tonight. Monday will bring its own share of chores." Hope smiled. She enjoyed the mundaneness of some tasks that allowed her a few quiet moments. She had a good book in her tote bag that she had been anxious to get back to. Saturday-night laundry sounded like a dream.

"I hadn't realized the baby shower would go so late," Mary said by way of an apology. But they both knew she was happy to have the business. Running a B&B in a small town apparently wasn't very lucrative, even though they were well into the leaf-peeper season.

And Hope was grateful for the job. Mary had offered it to her almost immediately upon learning she needed one. Hope feared the woman was just being nice so she wanted to make herself useful so she wouldn't change her mind. However, working in a B&B wouldn't have been Hope's first choice because each new guest brought the fear that someone might recognize her as Harper Miller from the suburbs of Buffalo. A woman who needed to stay missing.

Hope—she had trained herself to think of herself by that name, for fear she'd slip up or not respond to someone's call (which had happened far too many times than she cared to admit)—hadn't been able to see the evil until it was almost too late.

Almost.

Her tongue touched her bottom lip, a subconscious gesture whenever she thought of the beating she had taken. She shoved the thoughts aside. She was here. Alive. Out of reach.

New name. New hair color. New life.

"Would you like company?" Mary Lapp asked. "I'm not sure how I feel about you going into town so late. Alone." "I'm sure Ada wouldn't mind going with you." Eighteen-year-old Ada was Mary's youngest child, the only one not yet married off. They started the B&B two years ago after Mary's husband died and farming became too difficult. Mary seemed suited to it and Ada was chatty and generally agreeable with all the guests.

"It's eight p.m. in Hunters Ridge." Hope tried to sound like Mary's concern was the most ridiculous thing she had ever heard. The string of the laundry bag dug into her shoulder, so she plunked it back down at her feet.

"Ada should stay here. She can help you tidy up." Hope smiled and hoisted the bag but didn't throw it over her shoulder. "I've got this."

"If you're sure."

"I am."

Mary pressed her lips together, seeming resigned. "Make sure you take your cell phone and call if you need anything. It's so dark out already."

"Will do." Hope pushed open the door and bumped the laundry bag out onto the porch. She ran back inside and grabbed the burner phone she had purchased. For emergencies only. She didn't plan to have any this evening.

Or ever again, if she had her way.

The husband from earlier had returned from loading up the baby gifts into his truck. The newlyweds had rented a room for the night. Mary would set out a buffet and Hope would make sure they had fresh coffee and anything else they needed while the mother-daughter team were at Sunday service.

"Need some help with that?" he asked when he apparently saw her widen her stance to steady herself.

"Nah, I'm good." Hope tightened her grip and took a step down the porch.

He tilted his head. "Humor me."

Hope had overheard that the baby was actually her new husband's dead brother's, but the brother had died tragically. When the surviving brother came to town to find out what happened to his brother, his brother's widow and he fell in love. Now they'd be raising the baby. It was definitely the fodder for rumor mills, and Hope hated that she knew all this information about him. It seemed like an invasion of privacy, but his wide smile and kind eyes suggested he didn't have a care in the world. Not today, anyway.

Hope set the laundry down and rocked back on her heels, adjusting the small tote bag with her book and phone on her shoulder. "I'm in that van. The work one." She gestured to the white van with the B&B logo on it, an outline of a farmhouse and an Amish buggy. She jogged ahead and opened the door. The man placed the laundry inside the back. "Thanks."

"You're welcome." He waved, walking backward. "Have a good night."

"You, too. I suppose I'll see you in the morning. Be sure to let me know if you need anything."

"Will do."

She watched him jog back into the B&B where he'd join his wife and celebrate all their good fortune. A new marriage. A baby.

A fresh wave of loneliness washed over her. She stood frozen, staring at the pretty farmhouse. The evening's illumination gave the structure a warm glow. Inside, Mary was mopping the kitchen floor. Hope would do laundry ten times over mopping. A stiff wind whipped up and rustled the fine hairs that had escaped her neat braid. She glanced around to a darkness never achieved in the city. Only in the day could she see the field that had once grown corn and the thick woods beyond it. But now it was as black as the basement closet her ex once held her in.

Is someone out there?

Stop. She was safe. No one from her past knew she was in Hunters Ridge.

A surge of adrenaline made her rush to the driver's side of the van, yank open the door and climb in. At first it'd seemed odd that Mary owned a vehicle, because she didn't drive. But it soon became clear she was a smart business-woman who could find workarounds. Little Amos, a young Amish man who didn't blink at being called in the diminutive, had yet to be baptized so the church leadership didn't seem to frown on him taking odd jobs as a driver. And now Hope was available to do the same.

Once safely inside the van, Hope adjusted the radio to her favorite Top 40 station. She had missed the ability to stream whatever music she wanted whenever she wanted, but she decided this was a small price to pay for anonymity and peace of mind. She respected her employer and was willing to play by the rules for a job, which meant no technology that the Amish couldn't use. Except in her case, the van and cell phone.

Hope liked to believe her own dead mother had found her this job because it was a photo of Mary Lapp and Hope as a young girl on a trip to see the Amish that had brought her back here more than a decade later. Hope had always sensed the trip to Hunters Ridge held some significance for her mother, but sadly she passed a few months later without sharing what that might have been. However Mary claimed that a lot of tourists took her photo—which was against the

Ordnung—so Hope let it drop, not wanting to offend the Amish woman who had so willingly taken her in. Feeling nostalgic about the last summer with her mother, Hope kept the photo pressed between the pages of whatever book she was currently reading.

Hope had always found herself deep in thought when she drove. An animal of some sort darted into the fringes of her headlights and scooted just as quickly back into the fields that lined the dark country road, snapping her back into the moment with a jolt from tapping her brakes. Her heart raced and she flicked on the high beams and reduced her speed. She had heard horrible stories about deer jumping out and causing major accidents. The last thing she needed was to end up in some hospital, with no insurance, under an assumed name. Shoulders tense, palms slicked, and nerves rattled, she arrived at the Wash & Go on Main Street and tried to remind herself that a few minutes of quiet would be worth the drive.

Hope parked on the street in front of the laundromat and gathered her things quickly and rushed inside. She wasn't exactly safe. Sure, the lights were bright, but anyone could come in. And there was no one else around.

She tossed the laundry bag down next to a washing machine and dug for coins in her tote. That was what he had taken from her. Her sense of safety. Freedom. Even her identity. She had to force herself beyond her limited comfort zone to convince herself someday she'd work her way back to normal. Someday.

Whenever that was.

Despite the warm autumn evening, there was a chill in the air that followed her into the building. She should have grabbed her hoodie. She stuffed the tablecloths into three washers and started them up.

She settled into a hard plastic chair with her back to the

window. The fluorescent lights emitted a constant low buzz that could be heard above the *whoosh-whoosh-whoosh* of the washer. She opened the book and stared at the words but couldn't focus. She slid out the photo of her, her mother and Mary. Mary had always looked distracted in the photo, perhaps simply because she was unwilling to tell the tourist that it was forbidden to take her photo. Yet young Hope had a silly smile on her face while her mother's expression seemed anxious. For years, Hope had created an imaginary dialogue between the women, but it turned out they were strangers.

The memory evoked an unsettling feeling and the fine hairs on the back of her neck prickled to life. Hope glanced over her shoulder. Her hollowed-out expression stared back at her in the cloudy window. Across the street, the open sign on a small shop went dark.

She tilted her head from side to side, trying to ease the knot that was tightening between her shoulder blades. Unable to sit still, she got up and wandered the rows of washers and dryers. She had been here twice before to do her own laundry. She went to the bulletin board and read a notice for an available apartment. Maybe when she saved enough, she'd be able to get a place of her own. For now, she was grateful for Mary Lapp's generosity, providing a bedroom, one too small to rent out to overnight guests of the B&B.

Something tickled the far reaches of her brain and then grew louder. *Sirens.* All the blood drained from her face. The urge to flee nearly overwhelmed her, making her feel nauseous.

It's fine. It's fine. No one knows you're here.

The sirens grew louder. She moved to the back of the laundromat, away from the large windows.

No one knows you're here.

She sat down on the worn linoleum, leaning against a row of washing machines, and buried her head in her hands.

You're fine. You're fine.

The sound of racing engines grew closer with the persistent wail of the sirens. Tires screeched. Glass smashed. Metal skidding across dated linoleum.

Her entire body bumped forward. She threw down her hands and scrambled like a crab dumped from the net onto the deck of a fishing boat.

A scream ripped from her lips.

The lights flickered, then went off.

Trembling, she stood. Ignoring the shards of glass that had rained down on her, she turned around.

A pickup truck had crashed into the storefront, narrowly missing her. The driver's head was tipped forward against the steering wheel.

"Oh my..." she whispered; her entire mouth had gone dry. She picked her way through the broken glass, around the displaced washers, and over to the driver's side door.

"Step back!" a voice shouted from outside on the sidewalk.

Hope shifted, the glass crunching under her sneakers, to find a sheriff's deputy aiming a gun at her. Instinctively she held up her hands and fought the tears filling her eyes. Her heart thundered in her chest, making it nearly impossible to comprehend the deputy's commands.

"I was just doing laundry," she squeaked out, realizing even in that moment how ridiculous she sounded. "I didn't do anything wrong."

The deputy made his way into the destroyed storefront. The barely contained anger on his face made her flash back to her ex. The hatred in the eyes was all too familiar.

"Ma'am, are you okay?" he asked.

She swallowed and only mustered a nod.

"You'll need to step back," he ordered.

Hope complied on shaky legs.

The deputy slipped past her and yanked open the truck door. Still aiming his gun at the man, he asked. "Where is it?"

The driver lifted his head and tilted it back on the head-rest. A sly smile slanted his lips. "I don't know what you're talking about." His speech was slurred. If it weren't for the trickle of blood running down his forehead and cheek, he might have passed for someone waking up from a deep sleep. A sarcastic someone.

What's going on? she wondered as she tried to make sense of the scene.

Be brave, another voice whispered.

Hope stepped forward. Someone had to. "Doesn't he need medical attention?"

The deputy blinked, seeming to snap out of it. Just then, another deputy rushed in. "Let me take over. You see to the woman." The new deputy on the scene glanced around with wide eyes. "Anyone else in here?"

"No, no...I was doing laundry alone."

The deputy held out his palm. "Let's go outside where I can ask you some questions."

Alarm spiked her heart rate. Questions? She didn't want to have to lie to this man. But more than that, she didn't want her name in an official report that her ex could easily track.

Hope Baker had only recently settled into a new town and job. She didn't want to have to run again.

~

Dear Reader,

Thank you for reading* PLAIN INFERNO. *I hope you enjoyed it.

It seems Hope Baker has found herself in trouble even

though that's exactly what she was trying to avoid when she ran away to Hunters Ridge to escape her abusive ex. Pick up the next book in the **HUNTERS RIDGE SERIES: PLAIN TROUBLE.**

Happy reading,

Alison Stone

ALSO BY ALISON STONE

The Thrill of Sweet Suspense Series

(Stand-alone novels that can be read in any order)

Random Acts

Too Close to Home

Critical Diagnosis

Grave Danger

The Art of Deception

Hunters Ridge: Amish Romantic Suspense

The Millionaire's Amish Bride: Hunters Ridge Amish Romance

Plain Obsession: Book 1

Plain Missing: Book 2

Plain Escape: Book 3

Plain Revenge: Book 4

Plain Survival: Book 5

Plain Inferno: Book 6

Plain Trouble: Book 7

Plain Secrets: Book 8

A Jayne Murphy Dance Academy Cozy Mystery

Pointe & Shoot

Final Curtain

Corpse de Ballet

Bargain Boxed Sets

Hunters Ridge Book Bundle (Books 1-3)

The Thrill of Sweet Suspense Book Bundle (Books 1-3)

For a complete list of books visit

Alison Stone's Amazon Author Page

ABOUT THE AUTHOR

Alison Stone is a ***Publishers Weekly bestselling author*** who writes sweet romance, cozy mysteries, and inspirational romantic suspense, some of which contain bonnets and buggies.

Alison often refers to herself as the "accidental Amish author." She decided to try her hand at the genre after an editor put a call out for more Amish romantic suspense. Intrigued—and who doesn't love the movie *Witness* with Harrison Ford?—Alison dug into research, including visits to the Amish communities in Western New York where she lives. This sparked numerous story ideas, the first leading to her debut novel with Harlequin Love Inspired Suspense. Four subsequent Love Inspired Suspense titles went on to earn ***RT magazine's TOP PICK!*** designation, their highest ranking.

When Alison's not plotting ways to bring mayhem to Amish communities, she's writing romantic suspense with a more modern setting, sweet romances, and cozy mysteries. In order to meet her deadlines, she has to block the internet and hide her smartphone.

Married and the mother of four (almost) grown kids, Alison lives in the suburbs of Buffalo where the summers are gorgeous and the winters are perfect for curling up with a book—or writing one.

~

Be the first to learn about new books, giveaways and deals in Alison's newsletter. Sign up at AlisonStone.com.

Connect with Alison Stone online:

www.AlisonStone.com

Alison@AlisonStone.com

Made in the USA
Middletown, DE
29 October 2024

63548243R00104